## Elizabeth Ferrars and The Murder Room

**>>>** This title is part of The Murder Room, our series dedicated to making available out-of-print or hard-to-find titles by classic crime writers.

Crime fiction has always held up a mirror to society. The Victorians were fascinated by sensational murder and the emerging science of detection; now we are obsessed with the forensic detail of violent death. And no other genre has so captivated and enthralled readers.

Vast troves of classic crime writing have for a long time been unavailable to all but the most dedicated frequenters of second-hand bookshops. The advent of digital publishing means that we are now able to bring you the backlists of a huge range of titles by classic and contemporary crime writers, some of which have been out of print for decades.

From the genteel amateur private eyes of the Golden Age and the femmes fatales of pulp fiction, to the morally ambiguous hard-boiled detectives of mid twentieth-century America and their descendants who walk our twenty-first century streets, The Murder Room has it all. **>>>**

## The Murder Room
### Where Criminal Minds Meet

**themurderroom.com**

**Elizabeth Ferrars (1907–1995)**

One of the most distinguished crime writers of her generation, Elizabeth Ferrars was born Morna Doris MacTaggart in Rangoon and came to Britain at the age of six. She was a pupil at Bedales school between 1918 and 1924, studied journalism at London University and published her first crime novel, *Give a Corpse a Bad Name*, in 1940, the year that she met her second husband, academic Robert Brown. Highly praised by critics, her brand of intelligent, gripping mysteries was also beloved by readers. She wrote over seventy novels and was also published (as E. X. Ferrars) in the States, where she was equally popular. *Ellery Queen Mystery Magazine* described her as 'the writer who may be the closest of all to Christie in style, plotting and general milieu', and the *Washington Post* called her 'a consummate professional in clever plotting, characterization and atmosphere'. She was a founding member of the Crime Writers Association, who, in the early 1980s, gave her a lifetime achievement award.

# Furnished for Murder

Elizabeth Ferrars

An Orion book

Copyright © Peter MacTaggart 1957

The right of Elizabeth Ferrars to be identified as the author of this work has
been asserted in accordance with the Copyright, Designs and Patents Act 1988.

This edition published by
The Orion Publishing Group Ltd
Orion House
5 Upper St Martin's Lane
London WC2H 9EA

An Hachette UK company
A CIP catalogue record for this book is available from the British Library

ISBN 978 1 4719 0704 3

www.orionbooks.co.uk

# CHAPTER I

THE STRANGER who had knocked at the door lifted his hat and said, " Mrs. Jeacock? "

He was a short solid man of about forty. He had straight hair that had receded sharply from his temples, leaving a peak, like a cock's comb, jutting down in the centre of his heavy forehead. His cheeks were full and smooth and almost colourless. Between cheek and brow, his grey-green eyes looked as if they had sunk farther into his head than had somehow been intended, like crystallized fruit that have sunk too deeply into the icing on a cake. They were eyes that stayed empty and expressionless even while he smiled at Meg Jeacock.

She had come to the door in her apron, with hands still wet from the washing-up that he had interrupted. She held them out before her, red and moist, showing that she was too busy to listen, if he had come to sell her something.

" I was given your address by Stokes and Bascombe," he said. " I believe your house is to let furnished."

" Oh! " On a note of surprise, she let her hands fall to her sides. " Yes—that's to say, not this house, it's a cottage we own." She looked muddled and bewildered, not sure what she ought to do about it. Uncertainly she added, " Come in, won't you? I'll tell you about it, if you like."

She turned, untying her apron and dropping it on a chair in the narrow passage as she led the way into the sitting-room.

It was a long room with a low beamed ceiling and a log fire, recently lit, crackling but still giving off no heat, in a great old fireplace. It was a shabby comfortable room, with bulb-bowls wherever there was room for them, and a great many books.

1

" Do sit down," Meg Jeacock said. " Do you smoke? Will you have a cigarette? "

She was anxious and shy and overcome with perplexity at the right social tone to adopt with a prospective tenant. Picking up a box, half full of cigarettes, she held it out to him.

" My husband's busy," she said. " I don't like to disturb him when he's working. But I can tell you all about the place and show you over. Only it's awfully small, you know, and rather primitive, and not really furnished."

She took a cigarette herself and let the stranger light it for her.

She was a small woman of thirty-five, slender, neat and unobtrusive, with brown crisply curling hair that was parted in the middle and drawn back into a tight little knot. She had gentle brown eyes and small fine features. Her skin, naturally fair, had the biscuity tinge and the reddening on the cheekbones that comes from spending a great deal of time, all the year round, out of doors. She was wearing a green and red tartan skirt and red woollen jumper.

" The rent," she said, looking out of the window as she said it, finding it too hard to meet the man's eyes when she spoke of money, " is four guineas a week."

He nodded, as if he knew this.

" And really there are only two rooms and a tiny kitchen, with a bath in a sort of cubby-hole out of it."

" It sounds just what I'm looking for." He had a dull colourless voice. " I don't want a lot of bother."

" Are you by yourself, then? I mean, aren't you married? "

" No."

" Then you'd want someone to come in and clean for you, I expect. It isn't always easy to arrange that."

" I'm used to managing myself," he answered. " Is there a telephone? "

" I'm afraid not. But you could always use ours."

" The cottage is near here, then? "

" Oh, didn't I explain? It's really—at least, it used to be—a part of this house, but it was much too big for us—just my husband and me, you see—and such an awful lot of work. So we had the end partitioned off."

" But the cottage is self-contained? It's got its own entrance, and so on? "

" Oh yes, it's quite private. We even put up some quite high wooden fencing to give it its own bit of garden."

" I don't mind about the garden," he said.

" You don't? " She sounded sorry to hear this. " It's tiny, but it's really quite pretty. There've been lots of aconite and snowdrops and now the crocuses are coming, and even a few primroses. You don't care for gardens? "

" I'd have it kept in order, if that's worrying you," he said.

" Well, I shouldn't like it to get out of hand," she said. " With a house it doesn't matter so much, you can always put it right, but once a garden's got out of hand, it's so difficult to catch up again. How long would you want it, d'you think? "

" Suppose we talk that over when I've seen it."

But the same uncertainty that she had shown when she first brought him in still possessed her.

" It's really *very* small," she said, " and the furniture—well, to tell the truth, we only put in a few odds and ends so that we could call it a furnished cottage and be able to get rid of the tenants if they—if they weren't suitable."

He smiled. Yet as it had when he first greeted her, his smile accentuated, rather than lessened, the look that had remained in his grey submerged eyes—of not in fact regarding her at all.

" I understand that," he said.

" Of course, we might be able to lend you a few more things, if you wanted them—or have you some furniture of your own? " she asked him.

3

"I need only very little," he said. "All I want is peace and quiet for a while. If I can have that, the rest doesn't matter much."

"Oh, you can have that, as much as you want of it! Well then, let's go and look at it. Just wait a moment while I get the key."

She went out and hurried along the passage to the kitchen.

The breakfast-dishes, which she had been washing when the stranger arrived, were on the draining-board. An electric kettle, filled with water with which she had intended to make some mid-morning tea, was boiling furiously. Some crusts of bread, which she had put aside for the birds, were on the table.

First pulling out the plug of the kettle, she slipped on an old coat that was hanging on the back door, then she took a key from a nail on the wall, and gathering up the crusts of bread, went back to the sitting-room. But just before reaching it, she paused for a moment, listening.

From somewhere upstairs came the faint and uneven but more or less continuous sound of a typewriter. That reassured her and she gave a quick secret little smile.

As she led the stranger into the garden, she tore up the crusts and threw them on to the strip of lawn in front of the house.

"I'm late this morning," she said. "If you weren't here, they'd all be here, clamouring. But they get used to new people very quickly."

He seemed, however, to have no interest in the birds. She found this strange and regrettable.

Going on along the path, a paved path that led up to a small painted wooden gate, she saw the stranger's car, a new, small Jaguar, in the road beyond.

She exclaimed, "Oh, I forgot to say, there isn't a garage."

"That wouldn't matter much, if there's somewhere I can leave the car," he said.

"You really don't seem to want much."

" No, just somewhere I can stay quietly. I——" It was as if he had just seen that some explanation of his lack of needs might be necessary. " I've some work I want to finish." The flatness of his voice conveyed that he was leaving a great deal unsaid.

" So you *wouldn't* be staying very long, she said."

" We'll see, we'll see," he muttered and stood still in the road, looking back at the house.

It was a two-story house, built in the shape of an L, its walls of grey stone and its roof of moss-grown slates. It was the toe of the L, projecting towards the road, that had been converted into the cottage that was to let. The house stood about twenty feet back from the road, with its garden divided into two parts by a new high wooden fence. A big horse-chestnut, with large pale buds swelling on its twigs and crocuses dotting the grass under it, stood in the garden that belonged to the smaller cottage. A hornbeam hedge enclosed both gardens. Here and there at the foot of the hedge gleamed an early primrose.

Going ahead of the stranger, Meg Jeacock unlocked the door of the cottage and led the way into a square stone-paved room, which at one time had been a store-room. But recently a new slow-burning grate had been installed there and the walls had been painted cream. There was a rush mat in front of the fireplace, a wooden armchair with worn brown velvet cushions, a cheap gate-legged table in the middle of the room and there were two Windsor chairs drawn up to the table. The one curtainless window looked out towards the road.

"Very nice," the man said in his colourless voice, hardly troubling, so it seemed to Meg, to look around him.

She showed him the tiny kitchen and the even smaller bathroom leading out of it. Then she took him up the dark little staircase, which shot steeply upward out of what looked like a cupboard beside the sitting-room fireplace, to a door that opened into the only room on the upper floor.

This room had two windows. One faced towards the

road. The other, which was in the wall that projected at right angles to the house next door, overlooked the neighbouring garden. Neither window had curtains. The ceiling was low, with a thick, dark beam across it. The uncarpeted floor was of freshly stained boards. There was a divan bed, a cheap chest of drawers and a Windsor chair like the chairs in the sitting-room.

"You see," Meg said, "it really isn't furnished."

The man walked to the window that faced the road and stood looking out of it. He had thrust his hands into the pockets of his tweed overcoat, which, like his car, looked new and fairly expensive. He seemed to be looking for something from the window, though there was not much to be seen but the narrow road winding past the house and a ploughed field opposite, with a footpath that skirted it and disappeared into a small group of trees, still leafless except for the first faint misting of green on the larches.

Looking out, he asked, "How far to the village?"

"East Shandon? A mile and a half," Meg said.

"There's a house there called Shandon Priory. Is that right in the village?"

"No, it's on the river. Actually it's nearer than the village and by that short-cut there"—she pointed at the footpath—"it's only about a quarter of a mile. But it's muddy at this time of year."

He turned and took another look round the room.

"I'll take it," he said. "It's just what I want. I'll give you a cheque for three months rent in advance and I'll move in this evening. My luggage is at my hotel in Carringdon. I'll collect it and buy some essentials and attend to one or two things and be out here probably about six o'clock." He took a cheque-book and fountain-pen out of his pocket. "Shall I make this out to you or your husband and what's the initial?"

Meg drew her breath in sharply, startled at the speed of it.

"Oh, but . . ." she said.

" Three months rent at four guineas a week," he said.

" Yes, but . . ." The shy anxious look had returned to her face.

" References? " he said. " I'll give you my bank. And I can give you the names of one or two people, but they won't mean anything to you. I've been out of England for a long time and I'm out of touch with things."

" I really ought to consult my husband first," she said.

" All right."

" But he's busy now."

For the first time she saw some expression come into the man's face, She was not sure what the expression meant, but just for an instant something glinted disturbingly in his dull grey-green eyes.

She went on hurriedly, " You see, if it's only for three months . . . I mean, I'd thought of a year at least. We don't want the bother of continually looking for tenants."

" I didn't say I was coming only for three months." He uncapped his pen. " I'm giving you three months rent in advance because I can't do much in the way of references. Now shall I make this out to you or your husband? "

" To me—Margaret Jeacock. But still . . ." She stopped, seeing him writing. Still looking worried, she accepted the cheque when he held it out to her.

" I'll be back at six o'clock this evening," he said.

" I don't even know your name." She was trying to read the signature on the cheque, a bold scrawl, dashed off with a flourish, heavily underlined and quite illegible.

" Chilby," he said. " Gerald Chilby."

" Only we shan't be in at six o'clock this evening," she said. " We've both got to go out."

" Leave the door unlocked then."

" I suppose that would be all right," she said dubiously.

But as if the cheque that she was holding carefully between two fingers, waving it a little to assist the drying of the ink, were the flag of some modest private victory, she suddenly became brisk and confident.

Starting down the stairs, she said, " We could let you have some coal, till you've got some of your own, and I can tell the milkman to call in the morning, and the baker comes on Tuesdays, Thursdays and Saturdays— I'll get you a loaf to-day, if you like."

" Thanks," Chilby answered. " I'll be glad of that."

" I can spare you some blankets too, and some crockery. And you must let me know if there's anything I can do for you."

" Thanks," he said again.

" And you must meet my husband to-night—or perhaps to-morrow."

She went on chattering, thinking of more and more things that she could lend him and he went on muttering thanks from time to time until he had got into his car and driven away in the midst of one of her offers.

She stood in the road until the car was out of sight. Then she took another thoughtful look at the cheque, at the signature, which was like a deliberate exhibition of something violent and exaggerated in the very suppressed personality of the man who had been there, and at the sum of fifty-four pounds twelve shillings, for which the cheque had been made out.

Looking at the figures, her face lit up with a brilliant smile. She turned and ran into the house.

She went to the kitchen. Folding the cheque tenderly, she put it into her battered handbag, which was on the dresser, then, with a glance at the clock and, when she saw the time, a startled lift of her eyebrows, she snatched up a teacloth and started drying the cups and saucers that she had left on the draining board. As she did so, she hummed to herself in a soft excited voice.

By the time that she had put the crockery away, straightened the kitchen, made up the fire in the sitting-room, written a note for the baker and put it on the back doorstep, the time was half-past eleven. Putting on her

coat again and picking up her handbag, she went to the
bottom of the stairs.

" Marcus! " she called.

The sound of typing in a room upstairs continued for
a moment, then stopped.

" I'm going to Carringdon now," she called.

" Don't we get any tea this morning? " Marcus
Jeacock called back.

" I'm sorry, darling, I simply haven't had time and
I've got to go now to meet Kate's train."

" I thought it didn't get in till twelve-twenty-five."

" No, but there are some things I want to do before
I go to the station."

She heard some sort of an exclamation and then one
or two keys fiercely struck on the typewriter.

Letting herself out into the garden, she pulled the door
shut behind her and ran to the garage.

The Jeacocks' car was pre-war. Manœuvring it out
into the road, Meg drove at rather more than her usual
speed towards Carringdon, a small town about two and
a half miles beyond the village of East Shandon. By
herself, Meg was a more vivid person than she ever was
in the company of others. The diffidence, the uneasy
effort to please, that so often stiffened her features into
a set pattern of anxiety, disappeared then and allowed
her small weather-browned face to glow with animation.

She reached the car-park in the square in the centre
of Carringdon at ten minutes to twelve. Though that
gave her plenty of time to reach the bank before it
closed, she could not stop herself hurrying, as if there
were a risk that the doors might be shut in her face.

Running up the steps, she found the bank filled with
the usual last-minute Saturday morning crowd. Worming
her way through it, she found a pen and an inkpot and
wrote her name on the back of the cheque.

The sight of it gave her pleasure and she smiled at her
own small neat signature.

Then she took her place in the queue. Her air of

haste and of unusual excitement did not leave her until she had handed the cheque in over the counter and emerging again into the street, had turned towards the station where she was to meet the twelve-twenty-five from London.

# CHAPTER II

THE TRAIN, when it came in, was crowded. As the quiet station filled with hurrying people, Meg went to stand near the barrier, scanning the faces round her.

She knew that Kate Hawthorne would not be one of the first off the train. Kate would not hurry. In fact the platform had almost cleared before Meg caught sight of her, drifting idly towards her as if she were out for a stroll in the fields and quite unconscious of the people around her. Yet she seemed to have seen Meg before Meg saw her and as their eyes met she smiled a casual greeting.

This slightly bewildered Meg. She had been prepared to show some emotion at their meeting. She was also somehow troubled to see that Kate looked so little changed. This past year in London should have done something to her, Meg felt, should have smartened her, sophisticated her, taken some of the strayed wood-nymph quality out of her.

But there she was, wearing the same old camelhair coat in which she had been seen off by Meg and Marcus a year before, with her fair fine-spun hair still in the same loose bob, which, it was true, suited her, but was the way in which she had been wearing her hair for as long as Meg had known her. This was since Kate had been eleven years old and she was now twenty-six.

As she came to Meg's side, Kate slipped her arm through Meg's and gave it a light pressure, but did not speak until they had passed through the barrier and were free of the crowd.

Walking beside Kate, Meg saw that she had perhaps changed rather more than she had at first thought. Certainly her queer narrow rectangular face had become paler and she seemed thinner. But she had always been very slim, with a tiny waist and long narrow helpless-looking hands.

"Is your bag heavy?" Meg asked. "I left the car in the square, because it's easier to park there, but I could go and fetch it."

Kate shook her head. When they reached the street, she looked round her with an air of vague curiosity, as if this were a place that she had never seen before. The first thing she said had a sound of prim childish formality.

"It's very good of you and Marcus to have me, Meg."

"Haven't we been trying to get you to come for months?" Meg said. "I've missed you."

Kate gave her sudden wide smile.

"D'you know anything about why I asked to come?"

"Was there a special reason?"

"A special reason why it was just now. You don't know anything about it?"

"No. Should I?"

Kate gave a sigh as they started walking towards the square.

"I really don't know. But I've been worrying a lot and I thought you'd probably know all about it."

The abruptness of it all did not surprise Meg. Kate usually brought out immediately whatever was most on her mind.

"Is something the matter, Kate?"

"I suppose so."

"Something to do with the Priory? Or is it——?" Meg stopped. She had been about to ask if it was something to do with Roger Cronan, but she was not sure if it was yet quite safe to mention Roger to Kate.

"I'll tell you about it when we get in," Kate said.

Then for the first time, looking sideways at Meg, it occurred to her to ask, " How are you, Meg? "

" Oh, I'm fine," Meg said. " Fine. I've just let the cottage."

" For lots and lots of money? "

" That's how it feels to me."

" Money's wonderful," Kate said seriously. " It really is, isn't it? I mean the money you scrape together by being very desperate and very clever."

" I know," Meg said. " Fifty-four pounds, twelve shillings. I paid it into the bank this morning. The builders only cleared out on Wednesday and I let the place this morning—for four guineas a week to a man with a Jaguar, who offered me a cheque for three months rent in advance before I'd even thought of asking for it. Marcus doesn't know about it yet."

" Is four guineas a lot? " Kate asked. " I'm paying three for my flat, and that's supposed to be miraculously cheap."

" But that's in London. This is miles from anywhere and fearfully crude. We spent as little as we could on the conversion. We had——" She stopped herself in time. She had been about to say that they had had the advice of Roger Cronan, who was an architect, on how to set about it. " Marcus fought me tooth and nail about it from the first, but I'd decided something drastic had to be done and I pushed it through somehow. Poor Marcus. He hated the idea of giving up any of the house."

" I don't really like it either," Kate said. " I hate to think of changes happening, when one's got nothing to do with them. They make one feel so unnecessary. You know, Meg . . ." She put her suitcase into the back of the car. " I've been wanting to see you, but I haven't wanted to come back to Shandon."

" Perhaps this'll help you to get over that feeling."

" I don't think I want to get over it."

Meg backed the car out of the car-park and drove

along Carringdon's narrow main street. The Saturday
traffic was dense and she concentrated on it silently until
she reached the wider road that cut through the new
suburbs, which had spread out rapidly over what, a few
years ago, had been quiet meadows.

Only then she asked, " What is this trouble that I don't
know anything about? "

" It's a letter I had from Miss Harbottle," Kate
answered. " Is she all right, Meg? Isn't she getting at
all peculiar in her old age? "

" Good heavens, she's the sharpest old woman I've
ever known! " Meg said.

" That's what I'd have thought," Kate said, " except
that I've had the oddest letter from her. Among other
things, she says she's very troubled about what's going
on at the Priory and that it's urgent that I should come
to see her. I didn't want to, Meg. It's nothing to do
with me now, whatever's going on there. It isn't my
business. But somehow she made it sound as if I ought
to come."

Meg's forehead had crumpled into its usual anxious
frown. She blew her horn nervously at two cyclists who
were pedalling along side by side ahead of her, each with
a hand on the other's shoulder.

" Look at that! " she muttered. " As it happens, we're
going along to the Priory this evening for drinks."

" Oh no, Meg! "

" You see, I met Richard Velden in the village yesterday and he asked how you were. He often has since he
arrived, so I told him you were coming down for the
week-end and he immediately asked us all over there this
evening. Do you really mind very much? "

Kate gazed out of the window. The dreary little houses
of the suburb had been left behind and green fields spread
out on either side of the road. Here and there on the
hedges the sunshine caught a faint fresh shimmer of green.
The downs showed dim and blue in the distance.

" Not really—I'm not going to be difficult," she said.

" Don't worry about me. I don't really mind anything. Only I wish I knew what it was all about."

" Anyway, we needn't stay long," Meg said. " We can get there about six and leave about half-past seven. And he really seemed to want to see you."

" How do you like him? "

" I—I'm not sure. We haven't actually seen a great deal of him."

" Doesn't he want to know the people in the village? "

" Oh, I think so. It's our fault, probably. You know how immersed Marcus gets in his work and I've been terribly busy, coping with all the business of the cottage on top of everything else."

" So actually you don't really like him."

" I don't *know* him, Kate. I'm not going to say I don't like a person when I simply don't know him. And I haven't the faintest idea what Miss Harbottle's worried about. She hasn't said anything to me about it. It's true that there've been rumours . . ." But here, turning off the main road on to the road that sloped down towards the village, she seemed once more to be entirely concentrated on her driving.

They were passing a row of stone cottages with their little gardens enclosed by low stone walls. A group of boys in school caps were straggling along the road towards them, kicking a stone from one to the other. They scattered to the sides of the road, staring as the car went by. A thickset old woman, leaning on one of the garden walls, with an overcoat on over a blue apron, looked up sharply, then raised a hand in greeting. Through the bare branches of a grove of trees the grey walls of the church appeared for a moment.

" There are bound to be rumours in a place like this," Kate said. " You can't have a long lost heir turning up from nowhere without producing a crop of rumours. But they wouldn't worry Miss Harbottle, would they? "

" Did she say anything about rumours? " Meg asked.

"Not exactly. And even if there are rumours of

some kind, I don't see what they could have to do with me."

"That would depend on what they were."

Kate shook her head. She waited a moment, then shook it again. There was distress in her eyes, but there was stubbornness in the set of her narrow pale face, which was half-hidden from Meg by the fair hair flopping forward.

Slowing to take the turning towards her home, Meg said, "Anyway, you can go and see Miss Harbottle this afternoon and find out what it's all about."

"Does she know I'm here?"

"D'you mean you haven't let her know you were coming?"

Kate made one of her helpless gestures, as if to have notified anyone of her coming would have been to go too far along the road of practicality.

"Oh well, you can telephone when we get in," Meg said, " and fix up when you can see her."

But when they reached the house Kate loitered up the garden path behind Meg, standing still to look round her at the stretch of bright lawn growing ragged enough now to suggest that it would soon need a lawnmower, at purple and yellow clumps of crocuses and grey-green spears of daffodils thrusting through the grass. She stared interestedly at a robin that was pecking at the crusts on the lawn and when Meg reminded her that she ought to telephone, only looked vague and evasive.

Regarding the wooden fence and the budding chestnut tree beyond it, she said, " I don't know how you could bear to part with that tree."

"It was the only way to divide the gardens," Meg answered. "And you parted with lots of trees."

"They weren't ever mine," Kate said. " I never felt they were."

Meg's mouth tightened sceptically at this, but she did not reply to it.

That attitude of Kate's, she supposed, had supported

her as well as any other could have done, so there was nothing to be gained by explaining to her that her pretence deceived no one but herself. For there was no doubt that Kate must have believed for many years that she was to inherit Miss Velden's property, the house down by the river with the five acres of garden, and the fifty thousand pounds or so that would still be left even when death duties had been deducted.

Even though Miss Velden had never formally adopted Kate, but had only looked after her, first during her school holidays, while her parents had been in Malaya, and then entirely after their deaths there, while Kate's actual guardian had remained an uncle who took no interest in her, it had always seemed sure that she would be Miss Velden's heir.

But Miss Velden had died intestate and her property had gone to her brother's son Richard, whom she had not seen since he had been about thirteen, when his parents had emigrated to America.

Meg had no actual knowledge of what might have been done for Kate when this fact was discovered, but stuck to a conviction that something might have been saved if Kate had been willing to make the slightest effort to help herself. But she had been in a mood of bitter pride, incompletely masked by her vague light indifferent manner.

This had had far less to do with her financial loss than with the sudden reconciliation of Roger Cronan to the wife whom he had been divorcing. Eluding all forms of consolation and advice, Kate had even done her best at first to defeat the kind offices of Marcus, who, with an understanding of the situation which had rather surprised Meg, had spent one of his rare and always wholly distracting day in London, persuading his agent that she had an urgent need for a young and completely inexperienced girl in her office.

Taking Kate into the sitting-room, Meg hurried out to the kitchen, switched on the oven, popped into it the shepherd's pie that she had made earlier, came back and found that Kate had dropped her coat on to a chair and was standing with her back to the fire, looking round her with that air of mild curiosity which suggested that she had never seen the place before.

She was wearing an attractive light green woollen dress, close-fitting and very simple, and which had an air of expensiveness about it which Meg took to be a good sign. But still it did nothing to reduce what Meg thought of as Kate's lost-stolen-or-strayed look, the look of not belonging, of never having belonged to anything or anybody.

" Come upstairs now and I'll show you your room," Meg said, " then we'll have some sherry while lunch is warming up."

They went upstairs together.

The spare bedroom was at the end of the passage, a room that until recently had had a second door that led into the room beyond, which was now a part of the cottage. This door had been blocked up and the wall where it had been freshly papered.

The bedroom was a gay little room. There was a pale yellow counterpane on the bed and there were yellow and white frilly curtains framing the casement window. The window was open and a sharp little breeze stirred the curtains.

Kate went to lean her elbows on the windowsill. " It smells so nice after London," she said. " You know, I've had the feeling this winter would never end."

Turning her head, she looked at the window in the wall of the cottage, jutting forward at right-angles to her own.

" When does your tenant move in? " she asked.

" Sometime this evening. And that reminds me," Meg said, " don't say anything about that to Marcus, will you? I want to break it to him in my own way. I'll go and call him now."

She went along the passage, opened a door, gasped at

the dense tobacco smoke, said, " Kate's here and we're going to have some sherry," closed the door and went downstairs.

Kate followed her a minute or two later, but the sound of the typewriter, always dithering and uneven yet oddly remorseless in its tone, continued for at least five minutes after Meg and Kate had settled down with their drinks by the fire in the sitting-room.

Then suddenly heavy footsteps sounded overhead, a door banged, feet pounded down the stairs as if there were a train to be caught and the door of the sitting-room was violently flung open.

" Kate, Kate—where's Kate? " Marcus Jeacock cried fiercely, running into the room as if he were afraid that she was trapped in a fire there and that it was his heroic duty to rescue her.

He was a small man and was about ten years older than Meg, but was sometimes thought to be fifteen or twenty years older than she was. He had grey hair, a lined sallow face, rather loose flabby cheeks and large bright restless eyes behind thick spectacles. He was wearing a high-necked woollen sweater, oil-stained flannel trousers and felt bedroom slippers.

Clapping both hands on Kate's shoulders, he kissed her, looked round the room and cried in a voice of fear and desperation, " We're out of cigarettes! "

" We aren't," Meg said. " There are some in the box and there's a packet in my bag. Sit down and talk to Kate."

But he was incapable of sitting down. He had been sitting down all the morning and now he had to prance wildly up and down the room. Swallowing a glass of sherry at a gulp, he then appeared not be sure whether or not he had had any. Several times he asked Kate how she was and how she liked her job, then each time forgot her answer.

As Meg filled his glass for a second time, he exclaimed, " I meant to change! I thought I was leaving myself plenty of time—I meant to put on my brown suit and one of my new ties before Kate got here! Perhaps I should go and change now—what d'you think, Meg? Have I time before lunch? It's very rude to Kate to go about like this, I think I really ought to go and change."

"I've got over the shock of it already," Kate said. "Just let me settle down and get accustomed to it."

"And you can dress up properly for the party this evening," Meg said, "new tie and all."

"What party?" he asked.

"I told you," she said. "We're going to the Priory for drinks around six o'clock. And that reminds me, around six o'clock the new tenant's coming in. I told him I'd leave the door unlocked for him."

"Tenant?" Marcus cried. "What tenant?"

"The man who came this morning, the one with the Jaguar," she said.

"I don't know anything about a man with a Jaguar. What's been happening? Why doesn't anyone ever tell me anything?"

Speaking very slowly, as if she had already explained this to him half a dozen times, but failed to make him understand it, Meg said, "I let the cottage this morning to a man with a Jaguar, for four guineas a week, and he's moving in this evening at six o'clock. He's a very quiet sort of man and he wants the place so that he can finish some sort of work in peace and quiet. I dare say he's a writer like you. And he gave me a cheque for three months rent in advance, so that he could move in immediately."

Marcus gave her one of his wilder stares, but it changed, while he looked at her, to a sullen sort of admiration. He showed in that look that he knew she had defeated him. For if he had been allowed to see the tenant, if he had had the faintest idea that a possible tenant was in the neighbourhood, he would have been ready to defend the cottage from him at all costs.

He did not say this. Instead, in the disturbing way he

19

had, he put his finger straight on to the sore spot of worry in Meg's mind.

"Any man who can afford a Jaguar and no doubt many of the other pleasant things of life, yet who goes and pays you three months rent in advance for *that* cottage, at four guineas a week," he said, "is a crook. God only knows what we've let ourselves in for."

## CHAPTER III

THAT, NATURALLY, was not the end of it, though perhaps it might have been if Meg could have left the matter there. But because of the discomfort of her own misgiving, she would not let it drop and eventually it was Marcus who, towards the end of lunch, said that this must be very boring for Kate and that they might as well talk about something else.

After lunch he disappeared to his room again and did not reappear until Meg had called to him three times that it was time for him to change to go to the Priory.

Soon after lunch Meg insisted on telephoning Miss Harbottle. Kate herself continued to show an extreme reluctance to do this. Several times she murmured that she would telephone presently, but her presently promised to become later and later, while she and Meg sat comfortably gossiping by the fire, until at last Meg made the call for her.

Miss Harbottle at once suggested that Kate should have tea with her that afternoon. Apologising in her crisp voice for not including Meg in the invitation, the old lady explained that it would be best that the talk she wanted to have with Kate should be in private. Meg accepted for Kate, saying that she and Marcus could call for her on their way to Shandon Priory.

"Oh, she'll be going there, will she?" Miss Harbottle

asked quickly. " She'll be seeing Richard this evening? "

When Meg said that that was the plan, Miss Harbottle went on, " In that case, Margaret, ask her to come to see me to-morrow morning. I should like her to have seen Richard before I talk to her. That will be most convenient."

When Kate heard this, she said " And I don't suppose I'll even recognise him. A boy of thirteen—a rather horrid boy of thirteen—that's all he was when I last saw him. But he had a scar on his lip, I remember."

" He's got a moustache now," Meg informed her.

They set off for the Priory at about twenty minutes to six. Meg drove the car, with Kate sitting beside her. Marcus, wearing his brown suit, a pale green shirt and a hand-knitted tie of amber silk, was huddled sullenly at the back.

They were to stop on the way to pick up Mrs. Arkwright, whom Kate knew only slightly, since she had come to live in the village only a few months before Kate had left it. Thea Arkwright was a widow who lived alone in a small modern bungalow by the river, not far from the gates of the Priory. She was about thirty, an energetic, rather brashly handsome woman, with cropped chestnut hair and a habit of wearing tweeds, together with a good deal of heavy jewellery. Marcus did not like her, but Meg, without committing herself too far about her own feelings, said that they ought to be nice to her, since obviously she was lonely, or why else should she spend so many of the evenings when she was not busy about the affairs of the Women's Institute, the Drama Group, or the Produce Association, in the Rising Sun, quietly drinking double brandies?

When Marcus heard that they were picking up Thea because her car was having a dent taken out of the bumper, he laughed acidly and said, " Why can't she walk? The way she drives, she must have plenty of practice. Kate, this'll amuse you. Thea's working very, very hard on Velden. No subtlety about it—just goes straight for the goal, fifty thousand pounds and Shandon Priory."

" Marcus! " Meg said.

" Well, it's true," he said. " No one could have fallen in love with a mere man as fast as Thea decided to fall in love with Velden—anyway, not a case-hardened character like her."

" That's a revolting thing to say," Meg said.

" Meg doesn't like gossip," he told Kate with a cackle. " I do, I love it. It's the only thing that really interests me."

" He's the worst cat I know," Meg said. " And he gets things all wrong too, as cats always do."

" I haven't got this wrong," he said. " And I haven't got it wrong that Velden's mind seems to be too taken up with other interests to——"

" *Marcus!* " Meg's voice was louder than before. Her face had flushed bright red.

For some reason, Marcus accepted it this time, muttering something confusedly to himself and sinking into silence.

Kate had been only half-listening. Throughout the afternoon one thought had gradually been gaining a more and more obsessive hold on her, until by now she could hardly think about anything else. It was that Roger Cronan and also, of course, his wife, would be at the Priory, and that she would have to see and speak to them.

No one had told her that they would be there. It was a conviction that had come to her for no reason except that it would be the most painful thing that could happen to her. So it was bound to happen, that was all there was to it. No one had even mentioned Roger to her yet, but the thought of him, it seemed to her, had been in the air all day. The very avoidance of his name by Meg and Marcus had laid a heavy emphasis upon it.

Kate might perhaps have made things easier for herself by speaking of Roger without waiting for anyone else to do it first. Once or twice she had tried to do so.

But really there seemed to be nothing to say about him. She did not want to know whether or not his reconstructed marriage seemed reasonably happy. She did not want to know what sort of woman the wife who had returned to him was. None of the things that she might have pretended to ask casually seemed to her worth asking, and none of the other things seemed possible to put into words. So each time that she had nearly spoken of him, she had instead asked something about Richard Velden.

A pallid and usually listless boy, but with a wild temper that came as unaccountably as his fits of affection and generosity, that was how Kate remembered him, from the last visit that he had paid to Aunt Chris, as Kate had called Miss Velden, although they were not related. Not a boy whose departure to America had filled Kate with any regret, or who had left any strong mark on her memory.

Thea Arkwright's bungalow was a depressing little place, with blotched roughcast walls and a roof of pink asbestos tiles. But its garden ran down to the river-bank and its windows overlooked a lovely curve of the stream, straddled by an old stone bridge and with willows drooping over the water. From the day that she had moved into the bungalow, Thea had talked of moving out again into something less hideous, less jerrybuilt, less damp, but her efforts to do this seemed never to have been serious, for when it came to the point, she seemed never to have been able to tear herself away from the river.

She was waiting for them at the gate. Getting into the car, she gave Kate a firm, brief handshake, said she was glad to see her again, then at once began to talk about the reluctance of all the members of the committee of the Produce Association, with the exception of herself, to do any work about the mid-summer fête.

Driving on, they crossed the narrow stone bridge and turned in at the gates of Shandon Priory.

It was a curious building, vaguely ecclesiastical in design, but with battlements to give it a confusing impression of fortifications. Built of weathered stone, it looked from a slight distance as if it might be extremely ancient, but in fact it had been built in the middle of the nineteenth century, being the third building to stand on that site.

The original priory had been destroyed at the Reformation, and nothing of it now remained but three low crumbling walls, rumoured to have been a part of the kitchens. The ambitious merchant, ennobled by Queen Elizabeth, who had acquired the land, had used the stone to build himself a fine mansion on the spot and this in its turn had been destroyed by fire early in the reign of Queen Victoria.

The present moderate-sized house had been built by a retired Indian judge, lived in after his death by his two unmarried daughters, used during the first world war as a hostel for Belgian refugees, then bought at a low price and in deplorable condition by Christina Velden.

She had employed an architect to make the lofty rooms with their tall sash-windows as Georgian as possible. Then when the fires in the mock Adam fireplaces had entirely failed to warm the great icy rooms, she had installed what had turned out to be a quite inefficient central-heating system. In Kate's mind the house was always associated with the smell of paraffin, from the numerous stoves that stood about throughout the winter to keep the pipes from freezing.

The door was opened now, not by any servant whom Kate remembered, but by a slight young man of medium height, who was wearing a light grey suit of loose American cut. He was very pale. Even his eyes looked pale. His reddish eyelids seemed to have more colour than any other part of his face. It was an oval face, with a rather girlish cast, which might have been the reason why he wore a little moustache, though this did not in fact add any look of strength, since it looked almost as if it had been playfully stuck on for his own amusement. It was drab in colour, like his close-cropped hair.

This surprised Kate, for one of the few things about him that she thought she had remembered clearly was that Richard's hair had been a carroty red.

As she took the hand that he held out to her, she said at once, " You used to have red hair."

" Red? " he said. " Actually red? I only remember a slight trace of ginger. And that's one of the things that fade with age."

He had a soft pleasant voice, low in pitch, and when he spoke and smiled, the animation that came into his face, with its pale cheeks and red eyelids, gave it an odd clownlike quality.

" Perhaps my memory brightened it up a bit," Kate said.

" You've lengthened out," he said, " but otherwise I'm almost prepared to say that I'd recognise you any-where—once I'd been told who you were."

He laughed as he took her coat from her.

Thea Arkwright walked ahead familiarly into the drawing-room and the rest followed her, Kate bracing herself to meet with the blankest face that she could assume whoever might be in the room.

The effort was unnecessary. There was no one there.

Richard Velden poured out drinks, asking them in turn what they wanted. But to Thea, without any inquiry, he took brandy and soda.

She gave a laugh and said, " That's rather naughty of you, Richard. You shouldn't advertise quite so blatantly how much we've been drinking together."

" Haven't you done something to this room, Mr. Velden? " Meg said. She spoke with clumsy haste. After Marcus's remarks in the car it would have embarrassed her to admit that she had either noticed Richard's gesture or heard Thea's remark. " I don't know what it is, but it looks different somehow."

He looked round, his eyes dwelling on Kate, who had

crossed to one of the tall windows and was looking out at the familiar garden.

" I've taken out my aunt's harp," he said. " I don't play the harp."

" Neither did Aunt Chris," Kate said.

" She didn't? " The lips under the little moustache twitched in a smile that made his clown's face look mournful rather than otherwise. " That's a shock to me, in fact, a disappointment. I've been trying to convince myself that I remembered her playing the harp. It would have been a rather charming sort of thing to remember. And when I found I couldn't remember it, I deduced she must have started learning to play it in her old age. I found that also a quite charming thought. There's nothing so indomitable as trying to learn a new instrument or a new language in old age."

" There was nothing very indomitable about Aunt Chris," Kate said. " And she only kept the harp because it had been her mother's or grandmother's."

" In that case, perhaps I'll bring it in again," he said. " It's been haunting me, as a matter of fact. But I don't think it will if I know it never got played."

" There's no reason why you should keep things as they used to. be," Kate said.

She looked out of the window again at the long slope of the lawn, flanked by copper beaches and a monkey-puzzle tree on the one side and by the tall hedge that enclosed the orchard on the other. Down at the bottom, between gaps in the rhododendrons, the river shone.

Meg said, " If I'd been you, Mr. Velden, I'd probably have changed everything round straight away."

" She would," Marcus said forcefully. " I've only to glance the other way for a moment to find that she's whisked the piano from one room to another, given away my favourite armchair, auctioned off half my books, divided the house in half and settled half a dozen complete strangers in it, and all without consulting me on even minor points. I'm almost at the point when I'm afraid to leave the house in case she sells it, has it pulled down or converted into a maternity home in my absence."

" I expect that's what'll happen to this place," Thea said. " Someone'll turn it into a hotel or a nursing-home or something."

" Are you going to sell it then, Mr. Velden? " Meg asked.

He spread his hands wide. " I haven't any definite plans. I've just been giving myself a holiday, getting back the feeling of living in England. But I'm not even certain if I'm going to remain in England."

" I've told him he ought to sell it," Thea said. " What good is it to a man like him? He's only living in about three rooms, with that crotchety old couple in the chauffeur's cottage looking after him. And the rates and the upkeep of a place like this are enormous. If he wants to go on living in the country, and I can't really see his doing that much longer myself, what he ought to find is a house like yours, really attractive, small and easy to run."

" Not so small and easy to run," Marcus said, " that we haven't had the whole end of it chopped off for the sake of the few shillings rent we'll get out of it. How would you like that, Velden? How would you like to come out of your study one day and find that some man whom you've never set eyes on and who's almost certainly a crook, to judge by his reluctance to give references, had somehow hypnotised your wife into letting him have half your house, for God knows what dubious purpose? "

" You do exaggerate so," Meg said with a sigh.

Kate had begun to wander about the room. The feeling of the house had been stealing over her, a feeling which had in it a strange and disagreeable pressure on her nerves, and which produced in her an immense constraint. Remembering, she realised how often she had had the same sensation there, not so intensely perhaps, because habit had blunted her awareness of it, but still with a steady and oppressive power over her.

Looking at ornaments and pictures with which she had once been so familiar that she had hardly ever looked at them, she was unconscious of Richard's light-coloured eyes following her. She appeared for the moment quite withdrawn from the people there and on the track of some deep and private interest of her own. When presently, with her glass of sherry still in her hand, she drifted out through the door, it was as if she really had forgotten that there was anyone else in the room and that she was a guest in someone else's drawing-room.

Crossing the hall to the foot of the wide staircase, she went up it, then along a passage to a door at the end.

This was the room that had been her bedroom during all the time that she had lived at the Priory. In its way, it was a pleasant room, with its clear view of the river, its plain mahogany furniture and good carpet, though, for a child, it had been a sombre room. Indeed, only a book-case, filled with tattered books, suggested that it had ever been a child's room. The books were still there, ranging from *Peter Rabbit* up to Dumas and Dickens.

She had taken one down from the book-case, and wondering what had made her leave these books behind, was reading the inscription, " To Katie, from Aunt Chris, 1943," when she heard a step behind her.

" I talk to myself too," Richard Velden said, " particularly in this house."

She turned to him with a smile.

" This was my room," she said.

" I know, that's why I came looking for you here when you strayed out," he said. " I'm glad you did. I wanted a chance to speak to you alone."

He was looking at her intently, his reddish eyelids raised in a way that made his eyes look prominent and staring. She thought what a mask of a face he had, how little of him it gave away. When the mouth smiled it was as if he were playing a trick with it. Rather an odd trick too, that might have curious consequences, just as his moustache made her think of trickery of some sort.

Strolling forward, his hands in the pockets of his loosely-cut jacket, he went on, " I suppose you don't actually remember me at all."

" Hardly at all," she said.

" Then you don't expect me to remember much about you? "

" Of course not."

" Good," he said. " I think that'll simplify what I want to say."

" You know, I don't think there's any real need for you to say it," she said. " It's going to be something to do with Aunt Chris, this house and her money, isn't it? "

" You aren't afraid of being direct," he said. " I am, I find it very difficult. I always find it easiest to say what I don't mean. It's the result of being pushed around most of my life, or so I've been told. I'm inclined, myself, to believe it comes from a naturally tortuous character—if I can be said to have a character or even a positive existence at all. Wandering around in this house by myself, I've had my doubts. I've felt as nebulous as I must have been to my aunt. She didn't remember me either, you know. She left me all this only by an accident."

" No, that isn't true," Kate said.

" What d'you mean? "

" Well . . ." She thought over for a moment what to say to him. " People like Aunt Chris have a very great sense of family. I—I think she really intended to leave what she had to you."

He looked at her curiously, leaning his shoulders against the mantelpiece above the empty iron grate. Then he stirred with nervous impatience.

" I'm not getting on with what I meant to say. I told you I find it difficult to come to the point. And the point now is this. When I heard of my aunt's death, it seemed to me quite natural that she should have left all her property to me. So far as I knew, I was her only fairly close relative, and I only had the vaguest memory of you. To me you were simply a little girl who used to stay with my aunt. Do you understand?"

"Of course. You never thought of me as having any claims on her. That's quite simple."

"Yes," he agreed, "quite simple. It *was* quite simple."

"It's still simple."

"Oh no. Because since I came here, I've learnt what the real situation was. That's to say, that you were practically her adopted daughter and brought up to believe that you'd inherit all she had, or most of it. At the very least, that she'd make some provision for you."

"Yes, I did expect it," she said. "And when I—when I found I was wrong, it was a great shock. But I've got over it by now."

"It's the sort of shock I'd never get over," he said dryly, "and I shouldn't pretend to. No one would believe me."

"You can believe me."

"I was talking about myself."

"Oh, I like money too," Kate said. "I like it very much. But I've just been realising how very much I don't like this house and how I should have hated being burdened with it."

"The house represents money—ten or eleven thousand pounds probably, from what I've been told."

"So you're going to sell it?"

"What else can I do with it? D'you think it suits me? Do I look at home in it?"

"I can't think just where you would look at home," Kate said.

To her surprise, his white cheeks flushed. "I'm not sure what that means, but it sounds like a bad impression to have made," he said. "And I've still not got to what I want to say. It's this. If you'll tell me who your lawyer is, I'll tell mine to get in touch with him and to hammer out some sort of settlement that's fair to you. I'm not trying to pose now as planning to make some enormous sacrifice. I haven't got to the point of thinking in definite figures, and I'll add that if you'd been a different sort of person, I mightn't have suggested it at all. . . ."

At that moment, somewhere in the house, a telephone began to ring.

Kate, to her own great annoyance, had started to tremble.

" Oh no," she said, " no, it wouldn't be possible."

" Who is your lawyer? "

" I haven't got one."

From below, Thea Arkwright's voice shouted," Richard —some man on the telephone for you! "

Muttering something, and annoyed at the interruption, Richard went out. Kate followed him slowly.

She was still on the staircase a moment later, when a woman whom she had never seen before came quickly out of the room that in Miss Velden's day had been called the morning-room. She was a young woman, of about Kate's age, but taller and with tightly curling dark hair that framed a square, rather heavy but striking face. There was high colour in her cheeks and her eyes just then were brilliant with excitement. Breathing rapidly, she strode towards the door of the drawing-room, but catching sight of Kate, she stood still, staring.

At that moment Richard came out of the drawing-room.

An extraordinary change had come over him. The pallor of his face had become a sickly yellow, his lips were blue and his hands were out before him, feeling blindly for something to hold on to. He stared straight at the strange woman, but did not seem to see her.

She looked back at him incredulously. Then a change came over her too. To Kate it looked like a deliberate extinguishing of the excitement that had animated her.

Turning to Kate again, she said, " Richard seems to have forgotten to introduce us. You must be Kate Hawthorne. I'm Daphne Cronan."

31

# CHAPTER IV

AT HER WORDS, sense came back into Richard's staring eyes.

"I'm sorry," he said. He dropped on to a chair. "I don't know what came over me. I'm very sorry."

"You looked as if you'd just had an appalling fright," Kate said, coming down the remaining stairs.

Daphne Cronan gave a short laugh. "That's what I thought, but I wasn't sure if it was tactful to say so. Men don't usually run away in terror from mere guests."

He gave his head a shake, as if to clear it.

"I felt groggy. I don't know why. I'm very sorry."

The door behind him had opened. Meg stood there, looking concerned.

He looked up, saw her, smiled and said again, "I'm very sorry." Then he looked at Daphne Cronan. "I didn't know you were here, Daphne."

She gestured at the door of the morning-room. "I couldn't make anyone hear, so I came in by the french window. I'm sorry I'm late and I'm sorry Roger couldn't come. He telephoned from the office that he'd been held up."

As she spoke, she turned her wide dark eyes on Kate, examining her, frankly sizing her up.

Kate went on into the drawing-room.

Thea Arkwright, standing by the telephone and looking at it rather as if it were a dangerous animal that had somehow got loose amongst them, asked her, "Whatever came over Richard?"

He had followed Kate into the room. "Nothing—nothing at all. I need a drink. Who else is ready for one?"

Picking up the decanter, he went round the room, filling glasses.

His hand was not quite steady and as he filled Thea's glass, he sprinkled her tweed skirt with sherry. He did not seem to notice it and did not apologise. Looking at him thoughtfully, Thea absently mopped at the drops with her handkerchief.

Marcus was looking at Daphne with dismay.

She smiled at him and said, " Why, Marcus, what a pretty tie. Where *do* you get all your pretty ties? "

" I make them," Meg said, rather snappishly. Seeing Daphne, she had at once started making signals to Marcus that they ought to leave. She always expected Marcus to take the initiative in leaving any party. It was one of the things that she had never learnt to do and if someone did not help her, she was likely to find herself staying on and on, in more and more embarrassment, until an impossible hour.

" How clever," Daphne said. " I wish I was clever at something. Almost everyone else is. Miss Hawthorne, what are you clever at? "

Thea answered, " Clever at times at keeping her mouth shut. It's a trick you might try to learn."

Daphne, who was still excited, almost as if she had been drinking before coming, though that did not quite describe her state, gave a shrill laugh and turned to Richard.

" You shouldn't ask Thea and me at the same time, you know," she said. " Thea's always unkind to me."

He gave her a blank look, then looked down at his glass.

At that point Marcus, prompted by Meg's meaningful stare, said that it was time for them to be leaving.

As soon as he, Meg and Kate were in the car and Richard, with a wave to them from the doorway, had gone back into the house, Marcus slapped his knees and exclaimed, " In heaven's name, Meg, why didn't you say he was inviting the Cronans? I'd never have taken Kate there if I'd known."

" I didn't know anything about it," Meg said.

"And I don't think he did, you know," Kate said. "Anyway, it doesn't matter."

"Didn't invite them?" Marcus said.

"No," she said. "When he saw Daphne, he was surprised. I think she just came of her own accord, to take a look at me. Now we've got that over, things will really be easier, I believe."

"Well, I wonder which of those two will manage to outstay the other," Marcus said with a chuckle. He had offered Thea a lift back to her bungalow but had been answered with a smile and shake of the head. "That man exerts an extraordinary fascination over the women of the neighbourhood. Can you explain it to me Kate—if it isn't his fifty thousand pounds? Meg can't, she only gets scandalised when I point out the obvious facts."

"Don't listen to him, Kate," Meg said. "You know what he's like."

"I had a very odd talk with Richard," Kate said. Then, at what sounded like a tangent, added, "I wonder why he lives there."

"What was odd about the talk?" Marcus asked.

"Mainly that he was offering me money."

"He was? Oh, I'm so glad to hear it!" Meg exclaimed. "Then I've been right about him, saying that he'd probably be quite all right if one got to know him. Oh, I'm so glad about that."

"Hold on," Marcus said. "Don't you get swept off your feet as well." He paused. "I don't think Kate has been."

"I was so surprised," Kate said. "I didn't know what to think."

"But you'll take the money," Meg said. "If he's serious, of course you'll take it."

"Good heavens, no."

"Oh, Kate——"

"Money, money, money," Marcus cried. "Don't you ever think about anything else?"

"Not very often," Meg muttered fiercely.

"Well now, don't try to influence Kate," he said, "though it's true, if he *is* serious. . . . Was he, d'you think?"

"I don't understand it at all," Kate said. "I think probably he was just making a gesture of some sort, but the telephone rang before we could talk much about it."

"And that was queer, wasn't it?" Marcus said. "He came in to answer it looking quite normal, said hallo in an ordinary voice, then went dead white, dropped the telephone and staggered out of the room. But for just a moment, before he started to collapse, I saw his face." He tugged thoughtfully at his lower lip. "Yes," he went on, "that's how I've always imagined murder looked. Terror and violence."

"That's just Marcus's imagination running on," Meg said. "But still, it was very odd. I wonder what's the matter with him. His heart, I should think. Actually, he doesn't look at all healthy. Anaemic, for certain. Or his lungs, perhaps. I wonder if that's why . . ."

"Why what?" Marcus asked.

"Why he made Kate that offer. I mean, suppose he knows that he's seriously ill. That's a time when people start thinking of righting wrongs."

"I think it's just possible he was being honestly generous," Kate said.

"Or that he thought it might be useful to appear so," Marcus said, "when he felt quite certain, from all he'd heard about you, that you wouldn't accept his offer."

"That's a thing he couldn't be certain of," Kate said. "People are always unexpected about money."

"Like my dear Meg," Marcus said. "Would you think, to look at her, that she was avaricious, penurious, grasping, ready to pawn the very roof over our heads . . .?"

"Which reminds me," Meg said. "I expect Mr. Chilby will have arrived by now."

That he had was apparent before they had even gone

into the house, for there were lights in the upstairs windows of the cottage and the Jaguar was in the drive in front of the Jeacock's garage, leaving very little room for Meg to drive in.

This supplied fuel for Marcus's anger against the new tenant and when Meg at last succeeded in edging their old car into the garage, he exploded, " If he thinks he can leave his car there, he'll have to think again! Didn't I tell you we'd have trouble with him? "

" Well, you can tell him in the morning where you want him to put it," Meg said. " He just didn't know."

" He could have thought, couldn't he? He saw the garage, he might have supposed we'd want to be able to get our car in and out of it, mightn't he? "

" We have been able to," Meg said.

" It's a pure accident we haven't taken a lot of our paint off."

" The risk to his own paint was rather greater than to ours, I'd have said." Meg was locking up the garage doors. "Go and tell him about it now, if you like, then you can see for yourself what sort of person he is."

" I don't want to have any dealings with him whatever," Marcus said. " You let him into the place, you can cope with him."

They went on automatically bickering as they went towards the house.

Kate strolled in behind them, then went upstairs to her room. She had been thinking about Richard Velden, trying to place him in a world where he would not have seemed out of place, trying to guess how he had lived before he came to East Shandon, and suddenly a picture of him had formed in her mind in a frame that seemed to belong to it.

She imagined him, with his light graceful build, moving across a stage that was set as her old room at Shandon Priory had been set. She saw him leaning against a property mantelpiece, as he had leant against the mantelpiece there, and heard him, in his low-pitched clear and pleasant voice, speaking some very carefully rehearsed lines.

She found the picture singularly convincing. Deliberately invested in make-believe, he seemed to acquire a kind of authenticity. Had he ever been on the stage, she wondered.

She opened her door.

With a startled gasp, she stayed in the doorway, staring across the dark room. For a lunatic moment it seemed to her that a man was floating in the air outside her window, looking straight in at her. Also it seemed to her that he had a gun in his hand.

## CHAPTER V

IT WAS ONLY for an instant that the illusion persisted. As soon as she had got over the surprise, she realised what she was looking at.

One of the wooden-framed casements, divided into two large panes, was still open. Backed by the darkness outside, the glass was acting as a mirror, reflecting the interior of the uncurtained bedroom of the cottage. Gerald Chilby was not poised in mid-air outside Kate's window, but was in his own room, sitting squarely and solidly on a Windsor chair.

At once, when Kate switched on her light, the reflection vanished. She crossed to the window and closed it. At the appearance of the light in her room, the man next door must have moved, for she saw him now, standing at his window, looking towards her. She also saw, just before she pulled the curtains, that he was holding, not a gun but a pipe.

She said nothing about this to the Jeacocks that evening. But next morning, when Meg woke her, coming into the room with some breakfast on a tray and going to the window to pull back the curtains, Kate said, " You know, I don't usually sleep with my curtains drawn, but unless I do your new tenant and I can spy on one another."

She explained then the curious action of the window.

"Don't tell Marcus," Meg said at once, as she put the tray down on the table beside the bed. "He'd spend the whole evening sitting in here in the dark, keeping a suspicious eye on the poor man. I hope you don't mind breakfast in bed. I always treat my visitors to it, to keep them out of my way."

"*Mind* it!" Kate said.

"Well, stay there as long as you want to," Meg said as she went to the door. But with her hand on it, she paused. "You know, I do feel rather bad about having let the place to that man without consulting Marcus. But if I had consulted him, I know he'd have frightened him off. And he'd do his best to frighten off anyone else who came, until sooner or later I'd have had to let it without consulting him."

"So why not do it straight away? I think that makes sense," Kate said.

"After all, we do need the money," Meg went on. "Marcus works terribly hard and his books aren't doing badly, but prices go up and up, so we've either got to economise drastically, or find a way of making some more money. And to let the cottage only a couple of days after I put it in the hands of the agent, and for such a good rent—well, it seemed such luck, I couldn't resist it."

"I shouldn't worry about it if I were you," Kate said. "Marcus will get used to it."

"But you aren't a worrier," Meg said. "I am. I stayed awake half the night, worrying. And d'you know what I was worrying about?"

Kate shook her head.

"Well, just as I was going off to sleep," Meg said, "I had a perfectly horrible idea. And the more I thought about it, the more dreadfully convincing it seemed. I suddenly remembered, you see, that when that man was here, looking over the cottage, there were only two things he really seemed to want to know about it. One was how far it was from the Priory and the other was, had it a telephone? And then I thought of that call that came for Mr. Velden."

Kate looked startled. Then she shook her head again. "You've no reason to think it came from this man."

"But just think, Kate," Meg said. "Mr. Velden came into the room to take that call looking quite ordinary. He wasn't expecting anything private, or he'd have taken it in the morning-room. There's an extension in there, isn't there?"

"Yes."

"Well then, he'd have gone in there if he'd thought it was going to be something upsetting. But he said hallo, sounding quite cheerful and normal. And then as soon as the person who was ringing up told him who he was, that extraordinary thing happened—that sort of collapse. Just as if he was scared right out of his wits. And I've been thinking—well, it does hang together, doesn't it?"

Kate drank some coffee. She thought again of that first deceptive glimpse of the man in theroom next door, suspended outside her window, holding a gun. Only it had turned out not to be a gun.

Meg went on, "And I've been wondering if I oughtn't to get in touch with Mr. Velden and tell him about Mr. Chilby. Of course, by daylight it's all much harder to believe, but during the night I nearly went mad with worry. So just in case . . ." She paused, looking questioningly at Kate, her forehead wrinkled.

Kate said slowly, "Perhaps that's what you ought to do. It couldn't do any harm could it? Only suppose you wait till I've seen Miss Harbottle and found out why she's worrying about Richard. Wouldn't that be best?"

"Oh yes," Meg said quickly, "that's a good idea. And you could tell her all about it and see what she thinks. I don't want to be silly and hysterical, just because a man happened to want a telephone. Will you do that, Kate? Will you tell Miss Harbottle all about it and see what she thinks?"

Kate agreed to do this and Meg left her to finish her breakfast.

Kate did so and got up soon afterwards, dressed, made her bed, carried her breakfast tray downstairs and found Meg in the kitchen, making pastry for an apple pie. Marcus, reading *The Observer*, was by the sitting-room fire. When Kate appeared, he offered her the paper, but she told him that she was going out straight away to see Miss Harbottle.

" I'll drive you over then," he said.

" I thought I'd walk," she said. " It's a nice morning."

" Sure? That man's moved his car, we can get in and out without any bother," he said.

" Did he do it of his own accord, or did you ask him?" Kate asked.

" I asked him, but he was quite decent about it," Marcus said. " Told me he didn't know where to leave it, thought we'd call him when we got in if it was in the way."

" So you like him a little better this morning."

" No, I don't."

" What's the matter with him?"

" He's got a face like a damp boiled pudding without enough raisins in it."

" Is that all?"

" No, I think he's a crook. He's got practically no luggage."

" He may be going to fetch it from somewhere in a day or two."

" He didn't say so. He didn't say anything much. And when I spoke to him he looked all the time as if he were listening to bells ringing in his head."

" Perhaps that's what he wants the cottage for," Kate suggested.

" To listen to bells?"

" For peace and quiet, so that they'll stop ringing."

" Perhaps." Marcus grinned. There was no rancour in him this morning. He was protesting only to keep up his dignity.

Kate turned to the door, and went out into the garden.

There were bells ringing faintly in the distance as she started her walk. They were church bells from the village. The morning was fresh and bright, with more warmth in the sunshine than she had yet noticed that year. A blackbird was pouring out his song from the chestnut tree in the cottage garden.

*Greenacres*, Miss Harbottle's house, was in the centre of the village. It was a trim white house almost opposite to the church and mostly concealed from the road by a high dark hedge of laurel. A white gate opened on to a short weedless drive, which led up to a semi-circular porch, supported on columns. The door was dark green, with a shining brass lion-headed doorknocker.

When Kate knocked, the door was opened by a small round-shouldered old woman with a head that nodded tremulously on a wrinkled neck as she peered out at Kate through steel-rimmed glasses. She was wearing a black dress with starched white cuffs and had a small white apron tied round her waist.

" Oh, good morning, Miss Kate! " she said and held out her hand to shake Kate's. " It *is* nice to see you again. Miss Harbottle's very glad you're here. She told me this morning, ' Miss Katherine's coming,' she said, ' so I shan't be going to church, we'll have coffee, Maggie,' she said, ' coffee and biscuits, I expect she's got a good appetite,' she said. They're my own biscuits, of course, Miss Kate, that you always liked, and I can make them with butter now, which makes all the difference. They never tasted the same made with marge, though one had to do the best one could. You're looking very well, dear. Will you take your coat off, or d'you want to keep it on? I'd take it off if I was you, it's nice and warm in the drawing-room. I made up a nice big fire there, so you could sit and enjoy your coffee and your

41

chat. Miss Harbottle's very glad you're here, she's looking forward to seeing you."

By this time she had the door closed. Draping Kate's coat over a chair, she trotted towards the door of the drawing-room, still talking.

Maggie had lived with Miss Harbottle for thirty years. She had come to her first as a housemaid, in the days when Miss Harbottle had also employed a cook, a daily woman for the rough work and a full-time gardener. In the course of time the household had shrunk, Maggie's status changing as it did so and the two old women becoming very attached to one another. Each considered herself far younger and stronger than the other and was always fussing over the other's welfare. Maggie did the cooking and the housekeeping, Miss Harbottle vacuumed the carpets, weeded the flowerbeds and drove the ancient car. They did the washing-up together. A woman from the village still came in once a week to scrub and polish, and an old man, even older than Miss Harbottle and Maggie, came in for a day to mow the lawns and tend a few vegetables.

When Maggie announced Kate, which she did very formally, Miss Harbottle was sitting in a velvet-covered chair by a roaring fire.

Smiling, she said, " Maggie loves announcing visitors. It makes her feel so grand. Sit down, my dear. It's very good of you to have come."

She was a tall woman, slender, upright and free and vigorous in her movements. She was one of the women who are plain in youth, acquire distinction as they grow older and then eventually a kind of beauty. Her features were strong and expressive. Her white hair was short and was carefully and rigidly waved. She nearly always wore a pair of fine diamond ear-rings, to-day with a dress of limp and faded purple jersey.

Kate sat down and they chatted for a little while, until Maggie had brought in a silver tray on which were a coffee pot of Georgian silver, one white Utility cup and one of old Crown Derby and a plateful of home-made biscuits.

Pouring out the coffee, Miss Harbottle handed the Crown Derby cup to Kate and kept the white one for herself.

" Have you realised," she said, sipping the pale brown, very milky liquid in it without apparent discomfort, " that in a hundred years' time collectors will be hunting for cups like this, and arguing with one another whether or not they're genuine King George VI Utility. This one is, I believe. It survived our great nineteen forty-seven catastrophe, when Maggie and I both had 'flu at the same time—you remember that terrible winter—and dear old Fred Bunbane kept coming in to lend a hand—there was nothing he could get on with in the garden—and by the time I tottered downstairs again there was hardly a whole piece of china left in the kitchen. Now then, tell me . . ." She crossed her thin ankles on a footstool. " You've seen Richard Velden, haven't you? What did you think of him? "

Kate gave a smile and a shake of her head.

" You don't know? " Miss Harbottle said. " You haven't formed an opinion? "

" Why does my opinion matter? " Kate asked.

" Because you and he were children together. It seems probable that you would remember him more clearly than anyone else."

" But why does *that* matter? "

" Well, I won't beat about the bush. Do you think it conceivable that the man you saw yesterday could be an impostor? "

" Oh, I shouldn't think so," Kate said.

Miss Harbottle nodded her head. " You don't sound surprised at my asking you, however, so you've plainly asked yourself the same question already."

" Only because of your letter," Kate said, nibbling a biscuit. " It had to be about something, and that was one of the possibilities."

" And you aren't prepared to give a definite answer in the negative? "

" A *definite* answer . . .? " Kate's tone implied that this was something that she would at all times prefer to avoid. " You've just said that we were children together, but that isn't really true. Richard came on a visit once or twice. I can't tell you now how long those visits were, but my feeling about them is that they never lasted more than a week or two. And so my memories of him are very vague. The thing I remember most clearly . . ."

Miss Harbottle studied her thoughtfully as she paused, then said, " A not very pleasant memory."

" A horrid memory," Kate said. " I don't know what he'd done to annoy me, but I threw something at him, something fairly sharp, and it cut his face quite badly. He had to have a stitch in his lip."

" Then it must have been even unpleasanter for him than for you," Miss Harbottle said.

" I'm not sure that I agree."

" You were, I suppose, a quite violent little girl," Miss Harbottle went on. " But so many little girls are, and they don't seem to worry unduly about it. Still, it *is* upsetting to draw blood. There was a lot of blood, I suppose, and that left a deep impression." She seemed to find it surprising that Kate should have worried. " Did you scar him for life, I wonder? "

" He had a scar on his lip when I saw him last," Kate said.

" But he now has a moustache, so that doesn't help us."

" What's made you think that he possibly could be an impostor? " Kate asked. " After all, the lawyers must have checked up on all that very carefully. He couldn't just have walked in, said he was Richard Velden and taken possession of everything. He would have had to prove to them who he was."

" Yes, indeed. I've no doubt at all that they checked up most carefully. Nevertheless, there's a rumour about in Shandon that he's an impostor, a persistent rumour.

44

I don't know where it first came from. Maggie, naturally, heard it before I did, and continues to hear more of it than I do. But I find it very troubling, whether it's true or whether it isn't. If it's true, then we have a dangerous criminal in our midst. If it isn't, then someone we know is deliberately spreading a wicked falsehood."

" I believe you think it may be true," Kate said.

" I don't go as far as that. I admit I have a certain wish that it might turn out to be true. I haven't taken to Richard, who in some respects, it seems to me, is behaving deplorably. Which brings me to the second matter I want to discuss with you. It concerns Elsie Wibley."

" I realised he seemed to have got rid of her—or did she give him notice? " Kate said. " He hasn't got any servant living at the Priory."

" Well, that's his own business, and it was, I believe, Elsie who gave notice. She didn't fancy adapting herself to the ways of a new employer, she told me. So she went to live with her brother Ernest in that cottage by the ferry, of which, as you probably know, Richard happens to be the landlord. Ernest lived there all his life, Elsie lived there in her childhood and their parents lived there before them. Elsie, in other words, has simply gone back home in her old age."

" I know," Kate said. " Elsie sometimes took me to have tea there on her afternoons off, and Ernest used to let me help him work the ferry."

" Well, I don't know if you heard, Ernest died about six weeks ago," Miss Harbottle said. " He died quite suddenly, sitting in his chair by the fire. A terrible blow for poor Elsie, but she thought that at least she was quite secure, with the old-age pension, a few savings and that cottage at three shillings a week. And then, of all cruel things to do, Richard Velden gave her notice to quit."

" But he can't do that! " Kate exclaimed. " You can't turn a tenant out of an unfurnished cottage."

" I'm afraid he can," Miss Harbottle said. " She isn't

the tenant, you see. Her brother was the tenant. It seems that she has no legal right to the place at all and that Richard is perfectly entitled to turn her out."

"But why should he do that? What harm has she done him?"

"I don't suppose that comes into it at all. I imagine he simply wishes to sell the cottage. There's probably no deliberate unkindness in his action, but only a failure to understand the situation—to recognise, for instance, what home means to a woman like Elsie Wibley, and that it never once entered her head that she couldn't stay there till she dies. Really it's all Christina's fault. If she hadn't been so foolish about her will, she could have provided for Elsie, as I have for Maggie. Not that Elsie had been with her as long as Maggie has with me, but quite long enough all the same and been quite sufficiently good and reliable to have merited some consideration from Christina—and now from Richard."

"Of course, she *was* rather a problem," Kate said.

Elsie had been cook at the Priory for as long as Kate had lived there. She was a touchy temperamental woman, rather deaf and very sensitive indeed about her very plain cooking. Offending Elsie had been one of the worst offences in Miss Velden's well-meaning but rigid code of behaviour. When Elsie was offended she cried, got headaches and usually ended up in bed. She always prided herself on never taking offence, but once her feelings were hurt she exploded with such a great pent-up pressure of self-pity that she reduced the whole household to a state of terror.

"Of course she was a problem," Miss Harbottle said. "So are most people. And she was honest, loyal and worked for Christina for a very long time and that cottage is her home."

"Have you spoken to Richard about it?" Kate asked.

"No, I haven't. He doesn't like me any better than I like him. I feel instinctively that if I tried to approach him I should start to bully him—he's the sort of man who brings it out in me, like the last vicar but one. I deplore that side of my nature, but I've never been able entirely to control it. And what would make it particularly unfortunate in this case is that somehow I don't think it would *work* with Richard. He looks a rather weak and bloodless type of man, but gives me the feeling of having something inside him like a steel spring, that could uncoil suddenly and knock one right off one's feet. I shouldn't like that to happen to me."

" So you want me to speak to him."

" Yes, Katherine, I should be very grateful if you would do that." Miss Harbottle was one of the only people who ever called Kate by her full name. She also called Meg Jeacock, Margaret. Only Maggie was allowed the intimacy of an abbreviation. " He might have a sense of obligation to you which would incline him to do you a favour."

" And that's the main reason why you wanted to see me? " Kate said. " To try to get him to let Elsie keep the cottage, not to trap him somehow into showing whether or not he's an impostor."

" Doing the one doesn't exclude the other, does it? "

" I'm not sure. I mean, suppose he were nice about Elsie. . . . I think he was trying to be nice to me. He said he wanted my lawyer to meet his lawyer so that something could be worked out that would be fair to me. It may just have been talk—and it's true he used to have carroty hair, whereas now it's plain mousey—but still, if he's really quite nice . . ." She paused, noticing the startled gleam that had come into Miss Harbottle's eyes. " That does often fade, you know."

" Oh yes, it does," Miss Harbottle said. " I'd a friend once with the most wonderful auburn hair which had become plain mud-colour by the time she was forty. I admit it doesn't necessarily mean anything. But what I was really surprised at was the other thing you were telling me. This offer he made you—it really was an offer? He intends to share with you some of what he's inherited?"

"Oh, I don't know," Kate said. "I don't really want to know. I'd sooner leave it as it is." She stood up. "But I'll speak to him about Elsie."

Mrs. Harbottle gave her a shrewd look and seemed ready to leave it at that. Soon afterwards Kate said good-bye, and disentangling herself as rapidly as she could from Maggie, who came trotting out into the hall to open the door for her, started down the drive.

She was half-way along it before she remembered that she had not kept her promise to Meg to tell Miss Harbottle about the mysterious telephone call to Richard Velden, and to ask her advice about Gerald Chilby.

Kate might have gone back to correct this if at that moment she had not seen Roger Cronan standing at the gate.

## CHAPTER VI

THERE HAD BEEN some months in London when Kate had kept seeing Roger Cronan everywhere. In the street, in a tube train, in a Lyons teashop, she had caught sight, time and again, of a tall, slightly shambling figure, of dark hair, brown eyes and spectacles, and for an instant she had felt a complete certainty that this was Roger. Then her gaze had cleared and she had turned away, with a hammering of the heart, from the sometimes surprised glance of a complete stranger.

Thus, when she saw him at Miss Harbottle's gate, even though it was not surprising that she should see him in East Shandon, her first instinct was to deny his identity.

But this time his features did not alter as she looked at him. The high forehead, rather hollow cheeks and tense mouth retained the mould in which her imagination had cast them. The unsmiling gaze with which he watched as she approached him remained familiar. Only his face was more drawn than she remembered, as if he had recently been ill.

He looked, as she approached him, as if he were about to speak, but then he merely pushed the gate open. His car was in the road. He opened the door and Kate got in. He got in beside her, started it and drove along the village street.

He was driving towards Carringdon, away from the Jeacocks' house, but he had almost left the village behind before Kate said, " Where are we going? "

" Anywhere you like," he said. " Where do you want to go? "

" It doesn't matter," she said.

" I rang up the Jeacocks," he said. " They told me where you were."

" They're expecting me back to lunch," she said.

" There's plenty of time."

They were silent after that, Roger turning the car off the main road into a lane that led towards the downs.

Driving slowly, he brought a packet of cigarettes and a lighter out of his pocket and handed them to Kate.

" Do you want one? " she asked and he nodded.

She lit two and handed him one.

As he took it he said suddenly with extreme bitterness, " You didn't even want to hear what I had to say! "

" No, I didn't really," she agreed.

" Why not? Why couldn't we at least have talked? Would that have done any harm? "

" I didn't want to hear you explaining things that didn't need explaining."

" Didn't they? Why didn't they? Did you understand so much? "

" I understood that Daphne had come back to you and that you were going to let her stay with you."

He pulled the car to a stop. Crossing his arms on the wheel, he went on staring before him. Some ash from his cigarette floated down on to his sleeve.

49

" For God's sake, Kate, let me say I'm sorry—just that," he said, " and let me talk for a little."

She made a reluctant gesture of agreement.

" It's because our marriage isn't going to last much longer. I want to know if that means anything to you now." He turned to look at her sombrely.

She searched his face swiftly, then looked away.

He went on, " It can't last much longer. If it did, there'd be murder done—I'm not sure by which of us. And I've stopped thinking any more about whose fault it is. In the old days I put all the blame on Daphne——"

She interrupted, " This is what I don't want to talk about. I know all this. You were unhappy with each other, she fell in love with someone else, she left you, you fell in love with me, you told me you were going to divorce her, she came back to you, you told me you were going to stay married to her. That's the simple story and analysing all the stages of it doesn't make anything easier for either of us."

" It isn't the simple story. A story like that never is simple—don't you know that yet? "

" Oh yes—and yet at the same time it *is* simple. Really it was quite simple for me."

" Perhaps I'd have found it simpler if I'd had more courage," he said. " I know that's what failed. When she came back, I couldn't find the courage to tell her I wouldn't have it. It wasn't love, it wasn't a sense of duty, it was—just those ten years we'd been married. And it's a fact that unhappiness and a sense of failure can tie you to another person almost as much as love can. But now that's all finished. It's really finished. She's in love with Velden, and so the old story's started all over again, only this time. . . . This time even Daphne knows it's really the end."

He waited. He seemed to be expecting Kate to say something, but dropping her eyes to her hands, which were lying folded in her lap, she found that she could think of nothing that would not mean either far more or far less than she felt she could say.

After a moment, with a blundering movement, he started the car again, jolting it sharply, then sending it forward into a burst of speed.

" I'll take you back to the Jeacocks." His voice was hurt and when after a little she glanced up at him, she saw that his face was even more drawn than it had been while he waited for her at the gate.

Abruptly she said, " You know I saw Daphne yesterday."

" Did you? No, I didn't know that," he said.

" It was at the Priory. She spoke as if Richard had invited you both."

" He'd hardly have done that."

" She wasn't at all as I'd imagined her."

" You couldn't imagine what she's like."

His tone startled her. It occurred to her that this was the first time that she had heard him speak of anyone in a tone of such anger.

Not that he had ever spoken much of Daphne. But when he had there had always been an undercurrent of sympathy, as for someone whom he could not think of as wholly responsible for herself. It had made Kate visualise Daphne as dependent and rather helpless, holding him by her own continuing need for his care, an image that bore no resemblance whatever to the woman whom she had seen at the Priory.

In a way it was curious that Kate had never seen Daphne before that occasion. She and Roger had lived in Carringdon for three years before Daphne's temporary desertion of her husband. But it was not until Roger, recommended by Marcus, who was a friend of his, had come to the Priory to advise Miss Velden on some alterations in the house, that either Miss Velden or Kate had come to know him, and that had not been until a few weeks after Daphne had left him.

" Is Richard in love with her? " she asked.

" I don't know," he said. " I don't think that matters."

" Except that——"

" Listen, Kate," he interrupted, " I can guess what you've been thinking but haven't said yet. It's that this break that's coming may be no more final than the last one and that because of that I'd no right to try to see you or to say anything to you at all. That's what you do think, isn't it? . . . No, wait, don't answer. I only want to tell you that this time it will be final, as final as anything can be. But until I can prove that to you beyond the shadow of a doubt, I shan't make any attempt to see you again or to find out anything about your feelings for me."

" My feelings for you haven't changed at all, Roger."

" No, don't try to say anything. Not now."

" There's no reason why you shouldn't know that. You must have known it all along."

" How could I have known it? "

" But I don't think you'll leave Daphne unless she leaves you," she said. " I don't pretend I understand much about it all. I was out of my depth before and I think I still am. I've a lot to learn. . . . No, let me finish. I think perhaps if I were different, you could make up your mind more easily."

" It is made up."

She shook her head. " I don't think either of us is very strong or very ruthless. If one or other of us was, perhaps there wouldn't really be a problem. But we aren't—and I think Daphne is. And so, unless she's got Richard to go to——"

" No," he said. " Wait. Wait a little."

They had reached the Jeacocks' gate. As the car stopped, some catkins in the hedge happened to catch Kate's eye and later, when she went over what she and Roger had said to one another, she saw them again in her mind, yellow-green against the brown of the bare hedge, in the distorted yet lovely pattern that they always make.

" Oh, Kate! " Roger said softly.

She did not stir at once, then she turned to him, thrusting her hands into his.

" I could wait easily," she said, " if somehow I weren't frightened—I don't think only for myself."

Snatching her hands away, she tumbled out of the car and ran up the path to the house.

It was full of the smell of roast beef and boiled cauliflower. Marcus, who was in the sitting-room, called out something when he heard Kate but she ran straight upstairs. In her room she stood still, gazing round her, not certain that she might not start laughing or crying. Then in the mirror she met her own eyes. She went towards it and stood staring at herself with a look of strained questioning.

Presently she went downstairs. It irritated her at lunch that neither Meg nor Marcus referred to Roger. Such reticence now seemed ponderous and artificial. They questioned her about her visit to Miss Harbottle, but that Roger had telephoned to them to ask for Kate was a fact that appeared to have slipped their memories.

" She wanted to see you about that rumour that's around, didn't she? " Marcus said.

" Of course that's all nonsense," Meg said.

" Is it? " Marcus asked. " What do you think, Kate? Is it all nonsense? "

" Oh, Marcus! " Meg said.

" Meaning, as always, that I oughtn't to blow on the flames of gossip? Well, Kate, what do you think? "

" I think he's Richard," she answered absently.

The Jeacocks exchanged glances.

" That's a pity," Marcus said. " The other possibilities are so fascinating."

" Miss Harbottle also wanted to see me about Elsie Wibley's cottage," Kate said.

" That's what I thought she wanted to see you about," Meg said, " but I didn't like to speak of it in case I was all wrong. That's a dreadful business, of course. Someone ought to explain to Velden what it means."

" I've promised to speak to him," Kate said. " But I think I ought to see Elsie first, don't you? Would you mind if I did that this afternoon? "

" I'll drive you over," Meg said. " Then, if you like, I can take you up to the Priory afterwards and we can be back before Mr. Chilby comes in to sherry. Marcus relented towards him enough this morning to invite him."

" It's the best way to get some idea of what we're stuck with," Marcus growled.

Meg laughed.

" Ah," he said, " that's funny, is it? It's funny that our cottage is being used as a hideout for an escaped convict, or as headquarters for a confidence trickster, or possibly as a place to dump a lot of murdered bodies. I told you, didn't I, that when I went round to ask him to move his car, I saw at a glance that he'd moved in without any luggage? Or at most, just a small case. What sort of behaviour is that? "

" I expect the rest will come later," Meg said.

" And what will be in it? "

" That isn't our business."

" I should consider a trunk with a body in it, or say a machine for printing pound notes, most strictly my business."

" Well, you can tell him so when he comes in this evening. Kate, have some more apple-pie No? Then I'll make the coffee and we'll go out straight afterwards."

The cottage by the ferry, in which Elsie Wibley, her brother and their parents before them had lived most of their lives, was on the opposite side of the river to Thea Arkwright's bungalow and about two hundred yards downstream It was a white cottage with a steep thatched roof, small windows set deep in the thick walls and a low doorway. Its garden sloped down to the river and because it lay so low and was so sheltered, there were already daffodils out in the flowerbeds, while the forsythia, spread against the white wall was starred with yellow.

Kate had affectionate memories of the place, because of all the thick bread and butter and heavy currant cake that she had eaten on the riverbank on Sunday afternoons, and because of the excitement there had been in helping Ernest Wibley work the creaking old ferry.

This afternoon, when Kate knocked at the door, there was no answer. She knocked again. She knocked several times, then prowled round the cottage, trying to see in at the little windows, which were half-blocked with plants in pots and densely curtained in lace.

Returning to Meg, who was waiting in the car, she said, " It's no good. She's not in."

" We can try again later," Meg said.

Kate started to get back into the car. But just then she saw two children coming along the lane. They were aged about five and eight, had unkempt yellow hair and were dressed, the one in an overcoat much too large for her and the other in one that was too small. Each child clutched three or four primroses in a grimy hand.

Seeing the car at the cottage gate, they stood still and stared at it with patient curiosity, as if they were waiting for some show to begin.

Kate called to them, " Do you know where Miss Wibley is?"

Neither child made any reply. They went on looking at her, not with complete blankness but with so little sign of response that it might have been supposed that they had not heard her speak to them.

She tried again, " Do you know the old lady who lives here?"

Again there was no response on either face, then all of a sudden the elder child blurted out, " 'Er's gone to Carringdon, 'er goes Sundays to see Mrs. Walker, you can't never see 'er Sundays, not since Mr. Wibley died you can't."

" That sounds final enough," Meg said. " You'll have to try again to-morrow."

" But I'll have to go back to the office to-morrow," Kate said when she had thanked the children and got into the car. " I was going to go up on an early train."

" Wouldn't they give you a day to cope with urgent family business? " Meg said. " Get Marcus to ring up for you and ask."

" I suppose I might do that—if you don't mind. I mean, if you don't mind my staying the extra day."

" Kate, dear! "

" You see, I'd like to get the whole business wound up, so that . . ."

" So that you can shake the dust of Shandon off your shoes for good? "

Kate looked troubled, and did not answer. Meg drove home.

When they reached the house they heard the fitful sounds of the typewriter upstairs. This continued throughout the afternoon and even after the arrival of Gerald Chilby, so that Meg had to go upstairs to insist that Marcus should come down.

" I'm coming, I'm coming—in a minute," he said.

Meg made a face, knowing what that might mean.

" In a minute! " he repeated and banged out the next few words of a sentence.

Meg shrugged and went downstairs again. Marcus nearly always played this little game with visitors, to make sure, so far as he could, that they took him seriously as a writer, even if they never read his works.

Chilby, left in the sitting-room with Kate, had looked her over with much the same preoccupied stare that he had bestowed on the cottage the day before when he had been deciding to rent it.

" I think I've heard of you, Miss Hawthorne," he said.

Kate, preoccupied too, did not feel that this needed an answer. In recognising him, when he first came into the room, as the man whom she had seen reflected in her windowpane, she had wondered for a moment about the object that she had seen him holding. But since her meeting with Roger in the morning his image had come so persistently between her and any other face on which her eyes happened to dwell that in a minute or two she had almost ceased to be aware of Chilby in the room. She did not notice the curiosity with which his eyes, set deep in the smooth pale flesh, regarded her.

" I believe you used to live at Shandon Priory," he said.

" Yes, until about a year ago," she answered.

" You knew the old lady, then? "

" Miss Velden? Yes, she brought me up."

" A relation of yours? "

" No, a friend of my parents'." At that point Kate came out of her abstraction sufficiently to realise that there was something a little odd about such urgent questioning. For he had sounded hurried, almost as if he wanted to ask her as much as possible before Meg returned. " Why, did you know her too? "

" No." As soon as she looked at him, he looked down at his glass of sherry, rather as if he were wondering how he could have committed himself to drinking such a fluid. " No, I never met her. I've been out of England for years—Canada, the United States, South America."

That was when Meg came back. She overheard him.

" I've always wanted to travel," she said, " but my husband won't move an inch. He's a writer, you know, and that means that we might go to all sorts of places, but I can hardly ever persuade him to take even a day in London."

" Travel's over-rated," Chilby said.

" Then are you thinking of settling somewhere near? " Meg asked.

" I haven't any plans." He lifted his head, letting his little dull eyes settle again on Kate. " This Miss Velden," he said, " who died—she died suddenly, didn't she? "

" Quite suddenly," Kate said.

" What of? "

He had at last gained Kate's full attention. She glanced swiftly at Meg and saw that she seemed as startled as she was herself.

" Of flu," Kate said.

" There was a bad epidemic that winter," Meg said. " If you were abroad you wouldn't remember it. We all had it. My husband—he sends his apologies and he'll be down in a moment—followed it up with pneumonia. Of course they gave him penicillin and he recovered in no time. It's wonderful, isn't it? They can do such a lot of wonderful things now. If you think what it must have been like in the old days—I mean, before anæsthetics or even things like aspirins—you realise how immensely strong people must have been. I've just been reading the *Diary of Parson Woodforde*. . . . Have you read the *Diary of Parson Woodforde*, Mr. Chilby? "

Meg had put an enormous amount of effort into this change of subject. Her delicate little face was flushed with it.

" No," Chilby said. " Gastric flu, was it? "

" Yes," Kate said.

" That's what they called it at the inquest? "

" There wasn't an inquest."

" Oh, there wasn't."

" Of course not."

" I see. No, of course not, as you say. An old lady, a country doctor, everyone perfectly satisfied."

Kate looked at him stonily. She was just about to speak when Meg started again. " They really knew so little then—I mean in the eighteenth century. Parson Woodforde was always burying people, or going to visit sick people, or being awfully ill himself, but no one ever had the least idea what was the matter with them." As she was speaking, her gaze kept darting to the door. She wished that Marcus would come. He could be counted on to take charge of almost any conversation. " But it's a delightful book. You get so fond of all the people in it. They're so good to each other. They do so much for one another. And when the poor old parson dies . . ." She stopped. As if it had been bound to happen all along, she had somehow come back to the subject of death.

For the first time, she seemed to have roused Chilby's interest.

" He wrote about that himself, did he? "

" No, of course not," she said. " I meant, when the diary stops and he's an old man and very ill. I felt really sad about it."

" It would be interesting if people could write about their own deaths," Chilby remarked. He brought himself to drink a little sherry, then gulped the rest down, as if to get it over. " D'you know the present owner of Shandon Priory, Miss Hawthorne? "

" Only slightly," she said.

" He's a pretty rich man, I guess."

" Rich! " This at last was Marcus. A moment before there had been a heavy pounding of feet overhead and his customary rush down the stairs. He had burst into the room just as Chilby asked his question. " A rich man? A *rich* man? Who d'you think's rich nowadays, Mr. Chilby? "

He dashed to the table where the decanter stood, poured out a glass of sherry for himself, then noticed that Chilby's glass was empty and forcefully re-filled it.

" You've been out of the country, haven't you? " Marcus said, weaving swiftly up and down the room, decanter still in one hand, glass in the other and somehow not spilling any sherry. " Perhaps you don't know about income-tax. Or perhaps you don't know its full horrors. You haven't yet come up against the fact that the more you work, the less you get paid. I'm talking about the amount of work you do per hour. Do twice the amount of work, do you get paid twice the amount? No, you don't. For every extra hour you do, you get paid less. Does that make sense? "

He came to a standstill on the hearthrug with his back

to the fire. His bright, restless eyes fastened on his visitor's face. By an incredible piece of luck, from Marcus's point of view, he had been able, as soon as he entered the room, to introduce the subject that roused some of his deepest passions. Now, far from wanting to get rid of his visitor as quickly as possible, which had been his feeling as he ran down the stairs, he wanted to hold him there as an audience until the pressure of his own perpetual indignation had been relieved.

As Marcus went on, Kate got up quietly, murmured something to Meg and went out of the room.

She had a headache, which had been mounting ever since she had returned from her drive with Roger and she had some aspirins in her bag. If she did not take them soon, she thought, the headache would gain the upper hand and she would be laid out, helpless. Besides that, Chilby's questioning had disturbed her deeply. She kept thinking of Meg's guess that it was he who had telephoned Richard Velden the evening before and the more she thought about it, the more likely it seemed to her that that fairly wild guess had been right. She opened her door.

Across the room something moved.

She caught her breath, then realised that once more she had been tricked by the reflection in her own window of the interior of Chilby's uncurtained room.

Someone with an electric torch was moving about in it quickly, searching for something. For a moment all that she could see of the person was the hand holding the torch and the pale blur of the face above it.

Then, for an instant, she saw the face clearly.

# CHAPTER VII

THAT MARCUS, on the subject of income-tax, found his own anger and excitement rather enjoyable, was a fact of which he was perfectly aware, as he was aware of most of his own quirks. The lashing up of his own rage at a time when he felt certain that his audience was bound to sympathise with its excesses was a luxury to which he treated himself almost as deliberately as he might buy a bottle of wine. Yet the rage itself was entirely genuine, tending to make him even blinder than usual to what was going on around him.

He hardly noticed it when Kate left the room, or when, about a quarter of an hour later, she returned to it. He did not see, or at least, he did not let his attention dwell on the fact that Gerald Chilby's heavy face betrayed no glimmer of interest in the tangled and all-absorbing problems of expenses.

In a way, that was how Marcus preferred it. If Chilby had been too interested he might have wanted to do a little talking himself and this would have drained the pleasure of some of its richness.

Chilby stayed for three-quarters of an hour, drank two glasses of sherry, then in the middle of one of Marcus's intricate calculations got to his feet, thanked the Jeacocks in his uninflected voice and made for the door.

It took Marcus by surprise. It made him suddenly realise that his own glass was empty and that he badly wanted another drink, or probably several.

" That's the worst of this sort of thing," he said to Kate when Chilby had gone. " It just gets one started. Now I could go on drinking and talking for the rest of the evening. In fact, if I don't, I'll probably start feeling morbid and depressed. Anyway, it'll be much nicer to do it now that that man's gone."

He carried the decanter over to Kate and was about to refill her glass when he noticed for the first time since she had come in that her face was unnaturally white and that her eyes looked feverish.

" Anything wrong, Kate? " he asked. " You aren't feeling bad, are you? "

She shook her head, smiling a tight-lipped unconvincing smile. She put her hand over her glass to stop Marcus filling it.

He filled his own and planted himself on the hearthrug with his back to the fire. He realised that the week-end had been difficult for Kate, and it annoyed him that she should have been subjected to the strain of it. He thought of her as extremely fragile and defenceless, in which he was partly right, though there was exaggeration in his picture, and he would have liked to offer her advice on the important art of self-protection.

He was himself an immensely sensitive human being, always suspicious of other people, very easily hurt and easily upset by disappointments, and he had built up a complicated system of defences to help him keep life at arm's length. If he could, he would have initiated Kate into his system, but he knew that it was incommunicable.

Teetering backwards and forwards on his heels, he said, " Well, I didn't take to him much myself, but I suppose we've got to put up with him, anyway for three months."

At that point, the door was torn violently open and Gerald Chilby strode in.

He looked hardly the same man as the one who had sat passively allowing Marcus to talk about income-tax. His face had turned a sickly mud-colour with anger. His forehead and his cheeks looked swollen.

" Where's that girl? " he shouted.

Behind him Meg, who had been in the kitchen, appeared flushed and frightened.

" You! " Chilby said to Kate, advancing upon her. " What have you done with them? "

" Mr. Chilby! " Marcus said in a tone of outrage.

Chilby thrust out his hand to Kate. " Come on, hand them over before I call the police."

Kate looked at him helplessly, shrinking back in her chair.

Marcus caught hold of one of Chilby's arms. " Are you out of your mind? "

He tried to swing Chilby round to face him.

Chilby made a movement and Marcus felt himself shaken off and sent staggering backwards. He was not a muscular man and had never tried to be one. He had always lived a sedentary life and liked it. As he regained his balance by clutching at a bookcase, it occurred to him that the arm that he had grasped must have been made of steel.

But if Chilby had steel in his body, Marcus had high explosive in his temper.

" Get out! " he shouted at the top of his voice. " Get out of this house and get out of that cottage! I'm not letting anyone stay on these premises for a moment who speaks to a friend of mine like that."

" Your friend," Chilby told him flatly, " has just broken into my house and removed certain pieces of my property. In case you hadn't noticed, I'm behaving pretty well. I've come here to demand their return instead of going straight to the police. Now, young woman——"

" Get out! " Marcus shouted. " Get out or *I'll* send for the police and it wouldn't surprise me at all if they're very grateful to me for helping them locate you."

" Oh, Marcus," Meg murmured miserably, " do be quiet. Mr. Chilby, do wait a minute. There's been some mistake."

" There's no mistake," Chilby said. " You saw her go out, didn't you? I was sitting here, having a friendly drink with you and this *friend* of yours takes the opportunity to go out and break into my house and ransack my property. And you saw her come in, didn't you?

You saw something had happened, you saw she'd been up to something, didn't you? If you say you didn't, you're blind or lying."

" I went up to my room, Mr. Chilby," Kate said. " I didn't go near your house."

" Don't say a word, Kate! " Marcus said. " The man burst in here, where he'd just been hospitably received, and started to behave like a ruffian. Don't say a word till you've received—till we've all received—a full apology."

" You're probably all in it together," Chilby said. " Not that it'll help you. So you might as well hand it back, or I shall call the police."

" Call them! The telephone is at your service," Marcus said grandly.

Meg's soft voice broke in tremulously, " If someone has broken into the cottage, Mr. Chilby, and taken something, you can be quite certain it wasn't Miss Hawthorne. So won't you just tell us what happened? Has a window been broken? "

It seemed to calm him slightly. " Not a window," he said sullenly. " The door was wide open. And some things have been taken."

" You seem to be very afraid of telling us just *what* was taken," Marcus said.

" The door was open? " Meg said incredulously.

" Yes, the lock hadn't been broken," Chilby said. " A key had been used."

" A key? " she said in the same tone.

She and Marcus exchanged swift glances.

Chilby saw it. " So that means something to you," he said furiously. " If it wasn't this girl who got in, you know who it was. You hatched it between you. You got me down here to listen to your damned yap yap about taxes while one of your lot got into my room and ransacked the place. A lot that'll help you. You know I can get another where that came from."

" Don't you think it's probable," Meg said, " that you

didn't close the door properly when you came out, then the wind could have blown it open?"

"I'm damned sure I closed it properly and locked it and put the key in my pocket," Chilby said. "Whoever went in used a key."

"I am of the opinion," Marcus said, "that no one went in. A broken lock or window would lend some substance to your story, but as there appears to be no evidence whatever that anyone in fact broke into the cottage, and as you are so unwilling to name the articles which you claim were stolen, I am perfectly convinced that the whole story is a fabrication. And now, Mr. Chilby, I shall write you a cheque for the sum that you paid to my wife yesterday morning and I shall expect you to vacate the cottage before twelve midday tomorrow."

Kate started to say something, changed her mind and remained silent.

Chilby turned to the door. "Save your trouble, Jeacock. That cottage is mine for three months and I'm staying in it."

He went out.

Meg looked as if she were going to burst into tears. Marcus went on glaring at the door through which Chilby had just vanished, then in a surprisingly calm tone, remarked, "He really is afraid of the police, you know. That's interesting."

In fact, he was intrigued by the situation. Until a few minutes ago he had been annoyed with Meg for having planted Chilby in their midst, but now that Chilby had revealed a positively sinister side to his character, Marcus was ready to forgive Meg, to comfort her and to assure her that her unsuspicious nature had been villainously exploited and that that really was not her fault.

At the same time, he looked curiously at Kate. She was sitting with her head in her hands, her fair hair flopping forward over one cheek and her eyes lowered.

" Well, what did happen, Kate? " he asked after a moment.

Meg, who had been about to return to the kitchen, stopped in the doorway with a look of shock on her face.

" Nothing that Kate knows anything about," she said sharply.

" That isn't so, is it, Kate? " he said.

Kate shook her head, but did not look up to meet his eyes.

" Wouldn't it be best to tell us about it? " he suggested.

" I suppose so." She stood up, tossing back her hair and walking to the window. With her back to the room, she went on, " I told Meg this morning that when the window of your spare bedroom's open the glass acts as a sort of mirror, so that one can see what's happening in the cottage bedroom—that's to say, when it's dark outside and when there's a light in the cottage. And that's how it was when I went up there a little while ago. I'd a headache and I wanted some aspirins I'd brought. I went into my room and saw someone hunting round in that room with a torch."

" Who was it? " Marcus asked.

Kate did not answer at once, but at last she turned round and looked at him.

" I'm going to tell you," she said. " I thought at first I wouldn't, but it's your cottage and so I suppose it might be important for you to know what's happening. It was Daphne Cronan."

Marcus whistled.

Meg said, " I thought it might be Roger. As soon as that man said a key'd been used, I thought of him. He had a key when he was looking after the alterations, and he hasn't given it back yet. But really I didn't believe that there'd been anyone in there at all."

" It wasn't Roger," Kate said, flushing as she spoke. " It was Daphne."

" Are you absolutely sure? " Marcus asked. " After

all, if you only caught a glimpse by the light of a torch. . . ." He stopped, seeing the flash of anger in her eyes. " I'm not doubting you," he said.

" Aren't you? " she answered. " You see, this is partly why I didn't want to tell you who it was. It doesn't sound good when I say it was Daphne, particularly as it sounds so unlikely."

" I only wanted to know if there was any possibility that you could have been mistaken," he said.

" I wasn't mistaken," she said. " I went down and waited for her at the cottage door. When she came out I told her I'd seen her and suggested she should come in and explain to you what she'd been doing. She said she'd explain to you later."

" That sounds pretty calm! "

" Oh, she wasn't at all calm," Kate said. " I think she was frightened when she saw me and she got rather angry and abusive."

" But whatever was she looking for? " Meg asked. " D'you think she knows Mr. Chilby? "

" I suppose it's possible," Marcus said. " The question is though, what are we going to do about it? From the sound of things, Chilby's got every right to make a fuss. All the same, I don't like the idea of telling him who was ransacking his room. There's no doubt he can get pretty ugly."

" We could telephone her and ask for an explanation at once," Meg said.

" The telephone! " Kate said sharply.

Both looked at her in surprise.

She shrugged uneasily and said, " It's only an idea that came into my head just then. I was thinking of the telephone-call that upset Richard so much. You remember, Meg, you said you wondered if it mightn't have come from Chilby."

" What's this? " Marcus said. " Why should Chilby have had anything to do with that? "

" It was just a guess of mine," Meg said, " because the

only things he seemed to want to know when he took the cottage were whether or not there was a telephone and how far it was to the Priory."

" I see. And what's your idea about the telephone, Kate? " he asked.

" Only that Daphne just possibly might have listened in on that call," she said. " You see, she came in by the french window of the morning-room, I suppose when Richard and I were upstairs, talking. And there's an extension in there. When the telephone rang and Richard went into the drawing-room to take the call, she may have decided to eavesdrop."

" And because of something she heard, came to see Chilby? "

" Not to see *him*, to look for something he's got."

" Something the mere mention of which had given Velden an appalling fright." Marcus's face had lit up with interest. " You know, that all hangs together remarkably well. I shouldn't be at all surprised if you're right. And that means that Chilby's object in taking the cottage, which has been puzzling us all, is to blackmail Velden."

Meg gave a moan. " Don't say things like that, Marcus! Blackmail's almost as bad as murder. You'll be saying next that I've let the cottage to a murderer."

" It could, of course, lead to murder," he said judicially.

" But still, why should Daphne start poking around here, even if she did listen in on that conversation? " Meg demanded.

" Sheer curiosity," Marcus said, " or a desire to help Velden by stealing the evidence that Chilby's intending to use against him—or a desire to do a little blackmailing herself. What about that? "

Meg gave a shudder. " I believe you're beginning to enjoy it."

" I don't know Daphne at all well," he said. " I don't pretend to, but I believe she's an unbalanced reckless woman whose moral sense went into retirement at an early age and who would find blackmail a quite natural occupation."

" But that's all guesswork—all of it."

" Except that she was searching for something in Chilby's room." He shot a swift glance at Kate as he said it.

" I know you don't absolutely believe me about that, Marcus," she said. " Who d'you think it really was— Roger, Richard, Miss Harbottle? "

" Oh, I believe you, Kate," he answered. " But I've got a feeling there's something you haven't told me."

" Well, there's one thing I haven't told you," she said, " and that is that when I first saw that odd effect in my windowpane—that was yesterday evening, when we came home from the Priory—I saw Chilby in his room and I thought that he was holding a gun. Then a moment later I saw him at his window and I saw that he was holding a pipe. But since we're talking about blackmail and murder, perhaps it would be best to bear in mind that just possibly what he was holding when I saw him first really was a gun."

" That's going too far," he said. " That's piling it on. I can believe just so much. . . . All the same, suppose it *was* a gun! What in heaven's name ought we to do about it all? You know, I haven't the faintest idea."

" I think," Meg said, turning to the door, " I'll go and get supper."

" Then I'll take a turn in the garden and try to sort it out," Marcus said. " Call me when you're ready."

He went out into the dark garden and began pacing slowly up and down the lawn.

He often did this in the evening, in the darkness, and it did not occur to him that the spring night was cold. The stars were out in a cloudless sky and the dark shapes of trees pointed towards them without the slightest movement.

Marcus tilted his head slightly backwards as he

walked the familiar few paces to and fro in the garden, gazing upwards.

At first he tried very hard to think out what he ought to do about Gerald Chilby. Ought he to go to the police? Ought he to go to Richard Velden? Ought he to go to Chilby himself and demand an explanation?

The trouble was that when he tried to compose a speech to make to any of these people, it soon appeared that he had nothing to say except that he personally had taken a dislike to Chilby.

He could, of course, report Chilby's statement that someone had ransacked his room, but if Chilby himself did not choose to do so, why should Marcus do it for him? All the rest that he could say came from the statements and the imaginings of Meg and Kate.

Marcus's own imagination was extremely colourful and he was very easily carried away by it. This did not appear in his books, because in his books he attempted to be grown up and use his intellect and the painstaking results were rather pedestrian. But when he was thinking about the realities of his life, his mind immediately swarmed with wild fears and hopes, certainties of dark plots against him and brilliant and daring counterplots.

This was a state of mind which he both thoroughly enjoyed and took for granted, assuming the same mental processes to be going on in everyone else. A natural result of this was that he was almost incapable of believing the whole of what anyone told him, even when he regarded the person speaking to him as in general entirely honest.

So when it came to the point, he very seldom made up his mind about anything, because there was really no more need to make up his mind about other people's fantasies than about his own. Except when he took a decision on impulse, before he had had time to start thinking about it, the decision eventually taken was nearly always Meg's.

By the time that Meg called him in for supper, he was

farther from, rather than nearer to a decision as to what should be done about Chilby. He came in looking solemn and absent and anyone who did not know him would have thought that his mind was busy with the necessity of taking some important and difficult step. In fact, his private self was at that moment attending very solemnly indeed at the bedside of Richard Velden, who had been shot six times in the abdomen. Velden was just conscious and was muttering a few unintelligible words over and over again. Marcus, bending over him, was trying to hear, trying to understand the words mumbled through the blanched lips of the dying man. Only two made any sense and they came over and over again. Gerald Chilby.

Gerald Chilby, of course, had murdered Richard Velden and Marcus knew perfectly well why he had done it. Chilby and the man who had passed himself off in East Shandon as Richard Velden had conspired together and on some dark quayside in Chicago had murdered the real Richard Velden, weighted his body with lumps of concrete and pushed it into the water. Then the false Richard Velden had come to England, claimed his inheritance but had omitted to share the proceeds with his fellow-conspirator. Instead he had started to live a life of extravagance and debauchery in the village of East Shandon, seducing most of the women in the neighbourhood and at last casting his eye on the young innocent and beautiful Kate Hawthorne whom he had already defrauded of the money that was rightfully hers.

It was at that point that Marcus became involved in the story. His actual position was not clear, but he had some delightful quixotic and intimate relationship with Kate, on which the presence of the real Kate at the table beside him, eating cold beef and beetroot salad, did not in any way intrude. As it happened, the first intrusion of reality on to the scene of death came from the telephone.

Marcus put down his knife and fork and went to answer it.

He heard the voice of Roger Cronan.

" Sorry to bother you, Marcus," Roger said, " but is Daphne with you ? "

" Not now," Marcus said.

" She has been, then ? "

" I believe so," Marcus said. " She—well, she dropped in for a little while, I believe. I didn't see her. Is anything wrong, Roger ? "

" I don't expect so really," Roger said, but his voice sounded tense. " She told me she was going to see you and Meg and she took her car. I tried to stop her, because . . . Well, I tried to stop her, but she went all the same. And she isn't home yet. I don't suppose it's anything to worry about, but she didn't say anything about coming home late."

Marcus pondered, wondering whether or not to tell Roger about Daphne's visit. But all he said was, " It isn't really late yet."

" No," Roger said. " It was just because of Kate, of course."

" Yes, well, she's probably dropped in on someone else and stayed for a drink," Marcus said.

" Yes, I suppose so. Good night, Marcus."

" Good night. . . . Oh, by the way——"

" Yes ? "

" I don't know if you've heard, we've let the cottage to a man called Gerald Chilby."

" Congratulations," Roger said.

72

# CHAPTER VIII

THE NEXT MORNING Kate, after telephoning her office and getting the day's leave she hoped for, paid a second visit to Elsie Wibley's cottage.

This time she went on foot, by the field path, since Meg had the Monday morning washing to do. Kate found Elsie at home. She also was busy with washing, pegging sheets and pillowcases on to a line slung from a corner of the cottage to an apple tree, though for some private reason she had draped her oddly coloured underwear over a currant-bush, where it bloomed like great exotic rather wilted flowers.

She was a tall bony woman with yellowish skin and hair that had faded to a streaky yellow-grey. She did everything at high speed, with her sharp elbows jerking and an intense nervous concentration on her face. Seeing Kate come wandering in from the lane, as usual not hurrying and standing still by the gate to peer into a blackthorn bush, where a couple of hedge sparrows had started building a nest, Elsie went on fiercely pegging up washing, as afraid of having her attention distracted as if she were a philosopher, fearing to lose the thread of an argument.

When Kate approached across the grass and said, " Good morning, Elsie—how are you? " Elsie immediately put two clothes-pegs into her mouth to make an answer impossible, then hung up a towel, an embroidered antimacasar and two lace curtains.

Only then she said, " Good morning, Miss Kate, I'm so glad to see you. The kettle's just on the boil. I know you'd like a cup of tea. Yes, I *am* glad to see you." And she smiled broadly as she took Kate into the cottage.

The rooms were low, dark, very full of furniture and

very clean. There was a strong smell of soap, furniture polish and household disinfectant, together with the peculiar mustiness of old houses.

" I'd heard from Miss Badger you might be coming to see me," Elsie said.

Kate had to think for a moment before she remembered that Badger was Maggie's surname.

" It's good of you to interest yourself in my troubles," Elsie went on. " I've been beside myself since Ern died, as if losing him wasn't enough, but finding I was going to lose my home as well. I sit here of an evening and think and think and wonder whatever I'm going to do. It isn't that I've got nowhere to go, I can go to Mollie— you remember my niece, Mollie Walker, she's got a house in Carringdon, a real nice house, not an old place like this. She's got gas-fires in the bedrooms and an airing-cupboard and she's been ever so good, saying I can go there, but she's got three children and I never was one for children, besides it's not the same as having your own place and then what am I going to do with all my bits and pieces? I don't fancy selling them, not when I've had them all my life, and some of them things Miss Velden gave me and some of them things Ern made himself, and then though Mollie's so good I'd die sooner than be any trouble to her and though I'd pay my share and willingly work my fingers to the bone for her, it isn't fair on a young couple, that's what I think, always having an old aunt to look after. And so the only thing I can think of is to get another situation for myself, which I wasn't expecting to have to do at my age and not really feeling up to it, though I know I can still give satisfaction, because it isn't everywhere now you can find a good cook, who isn't wasteful and who doesn't think that the way to cook a good dinner is to open a couple of tins . . ."

The last sentence, spoken in a voice edging rapidly nearer to tears, might have gone on for ever if the kettle on the kitchen stove had not at that point begun to whistle so loudly that it penetrated Elsie's deafness and self-absorption.

She made the tea, put it on a tray and came back to the parlour. The moment she was inside the door, she began to talk again. She told Kate that soon after his arrival in East Shandon, Richard Velden had come to see her. She had been gratified, thinking that it was because he remembered her from the visits that he had paid to his aunt in his childhood. Also she had immediately hoped that he had good intentions concerning certain repairs to the cottage that were badly needed.

"But not him," she said, pouring out black tea and diluting it to an angry tawny shade with half a cupful of milk. "He looked all round the place, saying hardly a word, not asking me a word about Ern or even saying anything that I'd call suitable about his poor aunt. And then of course when I got the letter I knew what he'd been thinking all the time he was here, going up into the roof like he did, asking about the water and the drains. 'Drains!' I said. 'You don't find drains in cottages like these,' I said, so he goes pacing out into the garden, to see if there's room for a septic tank, and that's when I began to think, because it's one thing to repair a roof that's letting the water into your bedroom, but it's another thing to put in a septic tank, but even then I didn't guess what was really in his mind, not thinking that he'd forget the way I used to make little things for him special—cakes and biscuits and sometimes meringues too, without his aunt knowing—and the way Ern used to teach him to fish. 'Miss Kate doesn't forget that kind of thing,' I said to Mollie, 'but then,' I said, 'we all know Miss Kate, we know where she comes from, we know who she is,' I said. 'How do we know who this Mr. Velden is,' I said, 'if he is Mr. Velden? How do we know that?' I said."

"Just a minute, Elsie," Kate said loudly into the ear nearest to her. "You said, 'If he is Mr. Velden. . . .' Why should you doubt that he is?"

Elsie's eyes took on the evasive look that appears in the eyes of the deaf when they do not want to betray that they have not the faintest idea what has been said to them.

Kate repeated what she had said, still louder. This time she was certain that Elsie heard her, but the evasive look did not disappear.

" Well, you know there's talk, Miss Kate," she said. " You know how it is in a village, there's always talk. People will say anything."

" Who's been saying this, Elsie? " Kate shouted.

" Everyone's been saying it."

" But who started it? "

" How should I know? I'm not one to waste a lot of time talking. I'm not one who can't open her back door without trying to see into her neighbour's yard. I mind my own business and get on with my work, the way my mother brought me up to do. She never was one to let us girls stand gossiping at the corner when there was work to be done. She used to say to us . . ."

All the things that a long defunct Mrs. Wibley used to say to her daughters poured out over Kate's questions, bearing them away on a swift erratic tide and drowning them.

In a little while, promising Elsie that she would see Richard Velden and try to make him change his mind, Kate got up to leave.

From the cottage by the ferry to the Priory was only a short distance. Meaning to see Richard immediately and then probably return to London by an afternoon train, Kate walked along the towpath. She reached the gates of the Priory, but then saw something that made her hesitate, then turn away and go on towards the Jeacocks' house. What she had seen was Richard Velden and Gerald Chilby, walking up and down in the garden together.

When she reached the house she found a car at the gate and as she went inside, she recognised the voice of

Thea Arkwright, argumentatively raised, while Meg's answers came low-voiced and depressed. From upstairs came the sound of Marcus's typewriter.

As soon as Kate appeared in the sitting-room doorway, Meg told her, " I've just been telling Thea about Chilby and Daphne."

" And I've been telling her she's a fool to worry," Thea said. " If his cheque's good, I shouldn't ask any questions."

" That's what Marcus says this morning," Meg said.

" There's never any point in worrying," Thea said. " If I were given to it, I'd have landed in the booby-hatch long ago. Act first and if possible don't think afterwards is my motto."

" But suppose that *was* a gun Kate saw reflected in the window," Meg said.

Thea looked at Kate curiously. " D'you really think it was?"

" I haven't any idea," Kate said. " Anyway, Richard and the man Chilby are walking up and down in the garden at the Priory, looking quite friendly."

" You know what I think it's really all about?" Thea said. " I think that man's got designs of some sort on the Priory. He may want to buy it and turn it into flats or something."

" But that doesn't explain the way Mr. Velden behaved when he telephoned," Meg said. " I mean, *if* it was Mr. Chilby who telephoned. Of course we don't know that."

" No," Thea said. " But I'll tell you something about Richard. He's a very excitable nervous man. Very touchy too, very liable to flare up and walk out if you say the wrong thing. All temperament, in fact—just the opposite of me. Perhaps that's why we get on so well." She laughed self-consciously and Meg looked embarrassed, as if she thought that Thea was making a fool of herself.

" Nothing ever upsets me," Thea added. " I haven't a nerve in my body."

Kate had sat down.

" I've been talking to Elsie Wibley," she said. " She told me about Richard's turning her out of her cottage. She also mentioned the rumour that Richard isn't really Richard. I suppose you've heard it, Thea."

" Heard it! " Thea said. " My dear, I started it! "

As Kate and Meg looked at her, she burst out laughing.

" Oh, I didn't mean to, " I didn't know what I was doing. But you know what happens when I've got nothing to do in the evening and I'm sick of my own company. I go to the Rising Sun and have a few drinks. And if anyone talks to me I talk to him and then I wander off home again and finish up the evening with a detective story. But sometimes what I say after about the third drink isn't as clear-headed as it ought to be. I don't say I get drunk, but I do get a bit more imaginative than I am usually. Not that that was the trouble that evening. It was the other fellow who got imaginative, suggesting things about Richard and me. Meant to flatter me, I suppose. And I said something like, ' Ah, there are a few things I wouldn't mind knowing about Mr. Velden. He isn't all that he seems,' or something like that. And there you are. The story's floated."

" Does Mr. Velden know about it, d'you think? " Meg asked.

" Oh yes. I told him. He laughed like hell," Thea said.

Kate was looking at her thoughtfully. " What did you mean when you said that he isn't all that he seems? "

" Couldn't tell you, my dear. Didn't really mean anything. It was just something to answer when the man I was talking to was saying some damn' silly things about him. The only thing is . . ." She paused, thrusting one hand through her cropped chestnut hair. Her gaze, meeting Kate's, also became thoughtful. " Of course, he *isn't* what he seems, but I don't know what I mean by that except that he was once an actor, and like most actors, never quite stops acting."

" And you really believe," Meg said, " that that

remark of yours is the whole basis of that rumour about his being an impostor?"

"Well, I'd never heard it before then and about three days later I'd heard it from four or five separate sources."

"Who was the man you were talking to?" Kate asked.

"It was Bill Greenway."

That made Thea's explanation seem quite probable. Bill Greenway was a smooth young man who worked in an estate agent's office in Carringdon, spent a great deal of time in the pubs of the neighbourhood and had a passion for being in the know, for being able to report, with cunning hints at information obtained from influential quarters, what was going on behind the scenes.

"All the same," Meg said, "I suppose it *is* just possible . . . Or isn't it? I mean . . ." She stopped confusedly.

"Just what do you mean?" Thea asked.

"That there's some sort of truth in the rumour."

Thea's face suddenly reddened with anger. "For heaven's sake—I thought we were all joking! How could there be any truth in it?"

Meg gestured vaguely.

Thea went on fiercely, "If you're going to say that there's no smoke without fire, let me tell you that it's one of the commonest phenomena there is. Speaking simply from my own experience——"

"Oh," Meg interrupted her, standing up, "here's Roger! And something's wrong, from the look of him."

She went quickly out of the room.

Thea turned to Kate. "Don't tell me you think there's any truth in it, Kate."

Kate was looking intently at the door. "No, no—I wish people wouldn't go on talking about it."

"After all, you used to know him."

"I knew—not very well—a boy of thirteen. But it doesn't make sense that this man could be an impostor. He could be all sorts of other things, but that—that's such a silly story . . ." Kate's soft voice died away as Meg and Roger came into the room.

Roger looked straight at Kate. His face was even more haggard than it had been the day before  Besides that, he had not shaved and his hair looked as if he had forgotten to comb it when he got up. His eyes were red-veined and opaque, with smears of exhaustion under them.

" Roger says that Daphne hasn't been home all night," Meg said.

Thea exclaimed. He did not glance towards her. Across the room his tired eyes seemed to be trying to tell Kate something.

" He's afraid something's happened to her," Meg went on, as Roger himself said nothing.  " He's just been to the police. They've no report of any accident, but he still thinks something must have happened  He wants to know—about yesterday."

" She was here, wasn't she? " Roger said  " She came here to see you. Marcus told me on the telephone she'd been here."

" Yes, she was here," Meg said.  " That is—well, Kate saw her."

" Only Kate? "

" Yes, just for a few minutes," Kate said.

" Do you mean it was you she came to see? " he asked.

Before Kate could answer, Meg said hurriedly, " She came to see our new tenant, Mr. Chilby. Kate met her by accident."

" Chilby? " Roger said in a bewildered voice.  " I don't know of any Chilby."

Standing up, Thea put her hand for a moment on Roger's shoulder.

" I've got to go," she said.  " I'm sorry, but there's a Wives' Fellowship meeting in Carringdon this afternoon and I'm meeting some of the committee for lunch. But I'm sure nothing's happened to Daphne, Roger. I'm sure you've nothing to worry about."

He did not seem to hear her.

She caught Meg's eye, gave a shrug of her shoulders and went out.

Only when she had gone Roger looked vaguely after her, as if he wondered who she had been. Then he looked back at Kate.

" Tell me about it," he said.

She started to tell him how she had gone up to her room and seen Daphne's reflection in the window. After the first few words, Meg murmured that she would fetch Marcus and left them. As Kate went on, Roger sank into a chair watching her with tired incredulous eyes.

" There's no sense in it," he said, when she told him how she had recognised Daphne's face in the moving light of the torch as she went here and there in the room, searching. " Couldn't you have made a mistake, Kate? Couldn't it have been someone else? " He sounded as if he were trying to push away from him a problem too difficult for him to think out, rather than one that particularly alarmed him.

" No," she said. " I went down to the door of the cottage and waited for her. She was very startled when she saw me. She couldn't think how I knew she was there. Then she got angry with me and told me I'd better get away from Shandon. But I had a feeling— it was only a feeling, Roger, and I may have been all wrong—that she was hardly thinking about me at all while she was speaking. It was as if she'd had some violent shock and hardly knew what she was saying."

" Did you tell this man Chilby what had happened? "

" No."

" Why not? "

She coloured and did not answer.

He reached out a hand to her. She came towards him and put her hand in his.

" I needn't have asked that," he said.

" I told Meg and Marcus about it," she said, " and Meg told Thea."

" Thea? " He looked round again at the chair where she had been sitting when he came in. " She went off very suddenly, didn't she? D'you think that was because she knows something about Daphne? "

" I think she just felt she might be in the way."

" Kate, I don't understand any of it," he said.

" Don't you think . . .? Well, yesterday you told me that things between you couldn't last much longer."

"And she's simply gone away and left me again? That's what Thea meant, isn't it? But I don't think so, Kate. I'm quite sure that if she'd done that she wouldn't have left all her clothes behind, including a new fur coat that she was very proud of and her odds and ends of jewellery."

" What *do* you think has happened, Roger? "

" I spent all last night thinking she'd had an accident with the car," he said. " I telephoned the police several times. There weren't reports of any accidents that she could have been involved in. Then this morning I went in to the police station. There still wasn't anything. They asked me a lot of questions about her state of mind and so on, hinting at suicide. I told them I didn't think it was possible. But the fact is, Kate . . ." His voice cracked. " Here's something I never told you, I'm not sure why, except that I had a terrible sense of guilt about it. When she came back before and when I told her about you and that she and I had got to have a divorce, she tried to kill herself. I heard her moving about in the night and when I went downstairs I found her with her head in the gas-oven. That's what took all the courage out of me. I'd always known she was an uncontrolled unbalanced creature and even when I couldn't love her any more I always had the feeling that it was my job to look after her. . . . Later, of course, I realised that she'd never meant to kill herself at all and that probably she'd only turned the gas on when she heard me coming downstairs, but by then . . ." He ended with a shrug.

82

There was a silence between them, then Kate said, " I wish I'd known."

" You were so awfully young, Kate."

" Yes, I expect it was my fault."

" That isn't what I meant."

" And you think that now perhaps she's doing something of the same sort again, trying to frighten you."

" That's what one can't ever be sure about, don't you see? That it's only to frighten one. And now you've told me this story about her coming to see Chilby, I don't know what to think at all. It doesn't fit in anywhere."

" I think it just might fit in. There's something we discussed last night, Meg, Marcus and I. I know it was only an idea, without any real evidence for it, but at least it makes a kind of sense out of what's happened. You see, when Chilby took the cottage, there were only two things he really seemed to want to know about it. He wanted to know if there was a telephone and also how far it was to the Priory. Then when we were at the Priory that same evening, Richard had a telephone call that seemed to give him an awful shock. And a moment afterwards Daphne appeared, saying she'd come in by the french window of the morning-room. And there's a telephone extension in there and she was looking very excited. So suppose the call had been from Chilby and Daphne had listened in to it and heard something about Richard that startled her very much. And then suppose she came here, trying to find something out about Chilby, or to find something he'd referred to when he spoke to Richard. It doesn't explain what happened to her afterwards, of course, but it might explain why she came to the cottage."

He thought it over, taking off his spectacles and rubbing his eyes with the back of his hand. His eyes without the spectacles had a peculiarly defenceless look.

" It might." He put the spectacles on again and stood up. " I'd better see this man Chilby."

" I don't think he's in," Kate said. " I saw him with Richard in the Priory garden."

" I suppose I'll have to see Richard too. Possibly it's the first thing I ought to have done. But if she'd simply gone there it's unlikely she'd have troubled to conceal the fact. And in any case, I doubt——"

He stopped as the telephone rang.

Kate was looking at it uncertainly, not sure whether or not she should answer it, when Meg came running in.

The call was from Miss Harbottle. She wanted Meg, Marcus and Kate to have dinner with her that evening. Meg consulted with Marcus, who had followed her into the room, then accepted the invitation.

As she put the telephone down, Meg said, " I've told Marcus about it all, Roger."

" And I wish I could make some useful suggestion," Marcus said. His face looked solemn and responsible. He started walking excitably up and down the room, with his usual skilful weaving in and out amongst the furniture. " I wish now I'd told you more when you rang up last night about Daphne's visit here, instead of letting you think she'd simply dropped in on us."

" It wouldn't have made much difference," Roger said.

" I don't know, I don't know," Marcus said. " I blame myself. At the time I simply didn't want to worry you."

" I know." Roger turned to the door. " I'll go home now, I think, just in case she's turned up. If she hasn't, I'll call in at the police station again. And if there's no news, I'll come back and talk to Chilby."

His eyes went towards Kate, then he went out. She had the feeling that she had had earlier that he was trying to tell her something that he could not or would not put into words. But it was not any simple thing, such as that he loved her.

As Marcus went out with Roger, she suddenly felt the tears spurt in her eyes.

Meg stood looking at her with a distressed frown, twisting a handkerchief in her hands.

" You know he doesn't want to find her, don't you? "
she said. " That's why he's so fearfully anxious about
her."

# CHAPTER IX

IMMEDIATELY AFTER LUNCH Kate made another attempt
to see Richard Velden. She set off as if she were in a
hurry, walking fast until she was out of sight of the house,
then she sat down on a stile and smoked a cigarette.

She was not in fact in a hurry to see Richard, but she
was determined to be out of the way if Roger should
return in the afternoon to see Gerald Chilby.

She could not drag her thoughts away from Roger.
Her mind was again so completely filled by his image
that she hardly remembered why she was going to the
Priory. But resistance to her feelings for him had become
so much a part of herself that this set up in her a strain
that made her numb.

The afternoon sun had almost the warmth of a summer
day. The haze of leaf-buds on the hedges had grown
greener even since the day before. Sitting on the stile,
gazing idly across the sloping meadows towards Thea
Arkwright's bungalow and the curve of the river, shining
pale silver in the sunlight, passing under its humpbacked
bridge and out of sight amongst over-hanging trees,
Kate felt as if she had taken some strong drug that filled
her consciousness with shapes and colours but blotted out
the understanding that might have given them meaning.

She was smoking her second cigarette when Gerald
Chilby came along the path from the Priory.

He had a noisy walk, each foot thudding on the ground
as if he were trampling it in bad temper. But there was
no bad temper on his face. A little smile of satisfaction
touched his mouth. He had a switch of hazel in his hand
with which he was making sweeping cuts at the air

around him, as if imaginary heads were rolling on all sides. He did not notice Kate until he was almost at the stile.

She got off it so that he could cross over. He muttered thanks, but had one foot on it before he seemed to recognise who she was. He paused. For a moment he looked at her questioningly, then shrugged his shoulders and went on over the stile. Kate threw her cigarette away and went on to the Priory.

This time the door was opened by an elderly woman in an overall. She took Kate into the drawing-room where she was left by herself for so long that she began to think that the woman had forgotten to tell Richard that she was here.

She noticed that the harp had been returned to its corner and this, for some reason, surprised her. She wondered why Richard had bothered. She was standing looking at it and very lightly brushing a fingernail across its strings when Richard came suddenly into the room.

He seemed impatient and nervous, as if she had interrupted him in the middle of something, but he managed a smile.

" This is a surprise," he said. " I thought you'd gone back to London."

" I stayed to have a talk with you," Kate said. " I found it was expected of me."

" About what I said to you on Saturday? "

" We can talk about that too, if you like."

He came to her side and put his hand flat against the strings of the harp to deaden their faint twangling under Kate's fingers.

" D'you mind, I can't bear the thing," he said.

" Then why did you bring it back in here? "

" It seemed to belong here—and I don't use this room much."

" Do you dislike all harps, or just this one? "

" I've never thought about it. Up to now I've managed

to live without any harps in my life. Who expected you to come and talk to me?"

"Miss Harbottle."

He gave a rather loud laugh. Because his voice was normally soft and pleasant, it sounded strange.

"It means trouble, then," he said. "She hates the sight of me. Did you tell her about the nice offer I made you? Did you tell her I wasn't all greed and vice?"

"I told her about your offer."

"Dear Kate."

She frowned at him.

"I know, I know," he said. "I'm in a mood. A bad mood. Don't you ever get in bad moods, Kate? Doesn't anything ever ruffle your composure?"

"It's true you're in a mood," she said. "Perhaps I'd better go away and come back another time."

"Not on your life. What's the good of a mood without a victim?"

"Is that what comes of seeing the awful Mr. Chilby?" she asked.

"So you know Mr. Chilby? Oh yes, of course, you're staying with the Jeacocks. But why do you call him awful? He's a business man. He buys and he sells. He sells you what he happens to have and at his own price, but then you don't have to buy, do you? So what's awful about that?"

She wondered if he was aware of the hysteria in his voice.

"He accused me of burgling his room," she said, "which I thought was pretty awful."

"On such a slight acquaintance? Oh yes, that was awful. *Did* you burgle his room?"

"Whyever should I?"

"Then for a good enough reason you would commit burglary? Perhaps even other crimes?"

"Perhaps. The thing he wanted to sell you, Richard —did you buy it?"

" That was only a manner of speaking." He moved away from her, sitting down on the arm of a chair. It was only later that it occurred to Kate as curious that he had shown no curiosity about the burglary or the circumstances of Chilby's accusation.

" At the moment my mind's on selling, rather than buying," he said. " D'you know of anyone who'd like to buy a hideous old house, full of genteel Victorian ghosts who sing ballads and play the harp? "

" I've told you," Kate said, " that harp never was played."

" Oh yes, it was. In the dead of night my dear Aunt Christina used to get up and play the harp. I know she did. She must have. She does it still."

" What makes you hate her so? " she asked. " You do, don't you? "

" Why should I? " he said. " But you might. She played you a shabby trick."

" Not really. I'd let her down, you see. I'll tell you about it, if you like."

" Is there something about it that I don't know? "

" I think so."

He shook his head. " I think I know it all. Your friends have gossiped from time to time. Didn't you think they would? "

" Oh yes, but there's something most of them don't know. They think that Aunt Chris died intestate because she simply put off making a will. She didn't. She destroyed her will and telephoned to her lawyer, telling him that she wanted to make a new one, leaving everything to you. He told me about that. I don't think he mentioned it to anyone else here and I didn't either, because I didn't much want people to know we'd had a quarrel."

" Just a minute," he said. " It makes it better, does it, that she did this to you deliberately and not just by accident? "

" Of course."

" I don't get it."

" Well, we had a quarrel. Or at least an argument. It was just before she got ill so suddenly. It was about —about Roger Cronan. She told me that she disapproved of me very deeply, and begged me to break things off. That was before Daphne came back, of course. . . . Still, the fact is, you see, when Aunt Chris was dying I wouldn't listen to her. And so I've always felt she had a right to do what she did."

He looked as if he still did not understand her. But he was watching her intently, with his eyelids raised in the way that made his eyes look prominent.

" Then she told you that she was going to change her will? "

" No, but I wasn't surprised when I found that that was what she'd intended to do," Kate said.

" It's beyond me," he exclaimed. " I'd have been even angrier if she'd treated me like that than if she'd simply forgotten about the will. I haven't made a will myself and I don't intend to. I'm going to spend what I've got—except that my offer to you still stands. Or do you feel too guilty towards the old woman to take any of her money? Isn't that what's the matter with you? Haven't you got some idea that that quarrel you had with her killed her? "

She turned away from him, going towards the window. When she did not answer, he gave a laugh.

" What a thing is superstition! " he said.

She stood looking down the long green slope towards the river. " It could just be pride, you know. I've been a charity child most of my life and for a change I like the feeling of not owing anything to anyone. But your offer's kind and generous. It makes me wonder . . ."

" Well? "

" If you're ready to be so kind to me, what's making you so ruthless to poor old Elsie Wibley? "

He gave his knee a sharp slap and laughed again. His

laugh, harsh and loud, was the part of him that Kate liked least.

" That's what you came about then? That's what was expected of you? "

She turned back towards him. There was mocking amusement on his face.

" It *is* her home, you know," Kate said. " She thought she could stay there for the rest of her life."

" As she's told me herself, in words of one syllable and sentences three pages long," he said. " I can't stand the woman."

" That shouldn't really come into it."

" Why not? I never could stand her. When I was a child, she used to lose her temper with me, then try to buy me off by cooking me things I didn't want."

" So you remember her? "

" Of course I——" He stopped. The mocking humour died out of his face. Yet his next words, in a sober voice, were, " That's really very funny. You have to admit it's funny. I didn't realise you were one of the doubters. Don't you know how the story got around—the story that I'm not the real Richard Velden? "

" I wasn't thinking of that," Kate said. " I haven't believed that story for a moment."

" But do you know how it started? "

" Thea Arkwright says it was her fault. But it's nonsense, anyway. What I meant is that you don't seem to have any feelings at all for this place, or any of the people here, so it surprises me that you'll even admit that you remember Elsie."

" If you'd been dragged around the world as much as I was," he said, " you wouldn't have many feelings for the places you'd been in. First it was my parents, always looking for a place where they could fulfil some extra-ordinary dream of fortune and happiness. Then it was a touring company I got into. I was an actor, you know —very third rate. But now let me test your memory. Do you remember hitting out at me with a chisel? "

" Was it a chisel? "

He stood up swiftly and came towards her. He put his hands on her shoulders.

" It was a chisel," he said. " You gouged a bit out of me that I have to keep hidden with this damn' silly moustache."

" I'm very sorry."

" She's sorry. Just like that. She's sorry." He tilted her face up and kissed her quickly on the mouth. " That's forgiveness," he said and turned away from her, going to the harp and suddenly ripping his thumb across the strings. " All right, all right, the woman can stay. And I hope she walks into the river some dark night and drowns."

" Richard——" she began.

" I said she can stay! " he said loudly. " But d'you know what it means? I could have spent five or six hundred on that place, putting in a septic tank, splashing some paint around and turning it into one of those modernised cottages that I'm told have got so popular and then I could have sold it for something between two and three thousand. And who's to say when an odd two or three thousand might come in useful? As it is, she'll pay me her three bob a week rent and probably get behind in that, and I'll have to repair that roof at a cost of fifty pounds or so, and replace some rotten floor-boards, and so on—there'll be something every year or so—all as an act of charity to someone I don't even like. What's fair about that? "

" It isn't particularly fair."

" And since I don't mean to stay here, I'll even have to pay an agent to collect the rent. Had you thought of that? "

" I hadn't thought of any of it."

" But it's what you'd have done if Aunt Christina had left the money to you? "

She did not answer.

After a moment he said insistently, " It is, isn't it? "

" I think it's what you really want to do yourself," she said. " I'm not sure why you've been pretending you wanted anything different."

" No, I don't want to do it! " he exploded. " I don't want to do any of it. But what difference does that make? I haven't wanted to do half the things I've ever done. I'm one of those people who can't say no to anybody. Have you ever met any of them? They aren't nice people. They're dangerous people. They give way all along the line, they lead other people on to push them around— and then what do they do? That's the question." He turned and stared at her. " That's what you ought to think about."

" If that's how you feel about it——" she began, then changed her mind. " No, *even* if that's how you feel about it . . ."

" It's all right," he said with a shrug, as suddenly quiet as he had been violent. " How I feel about things never seems to have made much difference to what happened."

" I suppose that man Chilby was pushing you around somehow before I got here," Kate said. " I want to ask you something about him, Richard. It's an absurd sounding question—at least, it sounds absurd in East Shandon."

" There are a good many places where what sounds normal in East Shandon would sound more than absurd," he said. " What do you want to know? "

" Is he the kind of man who . . .? No, it sounds so silly."

" Then it's probably true."

" Well, is he the kind of man who carries a gun around with him? "

She saw him go tense. !His pale sad clown's face emptied itself of all expression.

After a pause, in a voice that had become thin and toneless, he asked, " What makes you ask that? "

" Because I think I saw him with one, though a

moment later. . . . Well, I couldn't be sure and I decided I must have been dreaming."

" Tell me what happened," he said.

She told him of the reflection that she had seen in her bedroom window when she had returned, with Meg and Marcus, from the Priory on the Saturday evening.

She half-intended, when she had finished, to tell him of what had happened on the following evening, when she had seen Daphne Cronan in Chilby's room. But when it came to the point she did not do so. This was for the simple reason that she found it extremely difficult even to speak Daphne's name to Richard, after what Roger had told her.

Though he had shown no interest earlier in what Kate had said about the burglary, he showed a great deal of interest now in what she told him about her glimpse of Chilby with what might or might not have been a gun in his hand. He asked her several questions to make sure that he was visualising correctly the relationship between the two windows and the way that her own open window had acted as a mirror of what was happening in the other room.

Yet at the end of it he only shrugged his shoulders.

" I can't answer your question," he said. " I simply don't know."

" But you do know Chilby."

" He came to see me this morning."

" Hadn't you ever met him before? "

" No."

He said it so flatly that she had no doubt at all that it was a lie.

That did not much concern her. In case what she had seen in the window had been a gun, she had given him a warning. That was what had been in her mind when she asked the question. She left soon afterwards and Richard walked with her as far as the stile on which she had sat to smoke a cigarette.

When she suggested that he should come the rest of the

way and have tea with the Jeacocks, rather to her relief he shook his head. But as she climbed the stile, he said, " I'd like to see you again, Kate. About all this . . ." He gestured vaguely in the direction of the house behind him. " You may be the person who could give me advice. And I need it. How long are you staying? "

" I'm taking an early train to-morrow morning," she said.

" To-morrow? Can't you stay a little longer? "

" I've a job," she said. " I'd have gone back this evening, only Miss Harbottle asked us to dinner."

" You and the Jeacocks? "

" Yes."

" That'll be a nice exciting evening! Well then, good-bye."

" Good-bye," she answered. " Thank you about Elsie Wibley."

" Always supposing I don't change my mind," he said and turned abruptly and walked off.

Kate stood where she was for a moment, watching him with dismay on her face, but when he had gone a little way, he turned and waved to her and she could see that he was laughing.

She went on slowly towards the Jeacocks' house.

She was half-way up the path to the house when she realised that something was wrong there. A loud and furious voice, which she recognised as Marcus's, came down to her from the open window of Gerald Chilby's room.

" I've given you back your money and I'm telling you to get out! " Marcus was shouting. " And if you don't go, I'll call the police to put you out. I don't know what sort of crook you are, but I don't want you in my house."

A quiet voice answered him.

Kate did not hear the words. But something in the tone of the voice shocked her as she could never have been shocked by Marcus's fury.

# CHAPTER X

MARCUS HAD BEEN in the garden when Gerald Chilby returned from the Priory. So had Meg. She had been pruning the roses, an occupation that absorbed her too completely for her to have been able to pay much attention to what Marcus, striding up and down on the lawn and smoking one cigarette after another, had been muttering.

Marcus was extremely worried. He had worked himself up into a state of believing that he was to blame for everything that had happened. Beginning at the point that if he had been earning more money, Meg would never have thought of carving up the house, he went on to charge himself with having neglected his responsibilities as a husband, inasmuch as he had left it to Meg, in what he thought of as her youth and her ignorance, to find a tenant for the cottage.

That she had been imposed on by the odious Chilby now seemed to Marcus somehow very touching and he longed to apologise to her and comfort her after her harsh experience with the wickedness of men.

From this point he went on to accuse himself of cowardice and supineness, in having failed to evict Chilby the evening before, after his insulting behaviour to Kate. Then came criminal shortsightedness, in having kept from Roger Cronan the truth about Daphne's visit. Then came other more nebulous failings in character and intelligence, as Marcus's memory led him back, step by step, to the point where he had been responsible for introducing Roger to Miss Velden.

That, Marcus believed, was when all the trouble had started. For if Roger had never met Miss Velden, he would never have met Kate and fallen in love with her. If he had not done that, Miss Velden would not have disinherited Kate. If she had not done that, Richard Velden would not have returned to East Shandon. If he had not done that, Gerald Chilby would never have come there to rent a furnished cottage.

And if he had not done that, Daphne Cronan would not have come to burgle his room and then vanish into thin air.

Not that Kate, or anyone else, had ever told Marcus that Miss Velden had deliberately disinherited her. It merely seemed to him a certainty, from what he had known of Miss Velden. That Kate herself was unaware of this belief of his was due to the fact that, for all his love of gossip, he had never mentioned it to anyone. He had only written a story about it. But that was different, particularly since the magazine in which it had appeared was one unlikely to be read by his friends.

Meg, of course, had read the story, but because in it Miss Velden had been metamorphosed into an old man and because the hero of the story had been an obvious portrait, not of Roger, but of Marcus himself, she had never dreamt of connecting it with Kate.

Brooding on his shortcomings and suffering acutely because of them, Marcus heard heavy footsteps in the road and the creak of the gate next door. Through the fence, he saw Chilby going up to the cottage. He heard the door slam.

Marcus had just been about to light another cigarette. Now he flung it on the ground and ground it into the grass with his heel.

" I've given up smoking! " he cried.

It made Meg start, so that her hand slipped and she scratched herself on a thorn.

" Whatever made you think of that? " she asked.

" We need money," Marcus said. " I'm going to make that man take back his cheque and I'm going to turn him out—but I agree, we need money. I'd work for it, but what's the good of that? Would you and I get anything out of it? The only thing is to save money. The money you save is the only kind that doesn't turn into dust and income-tax. I'll begin by giving up smoking. That's our worst extravagance. I smoke forty cigarettes a day, that's seven and eightpence a day, that's two pounds thirteen shillings and eightpence a week, that's a hundred and thirty-nine pounds ten shillings and eightpence a year. Very well, let's save a hundred and thirty-nine pounds ten shillings and eightpence a year and stop having tenants. If I'd done it sooner, we'd have saved ourselves and probably other people too a lot of trouble and distress."

" The only thing is, I don't think it'll work," Meg said.

" Why not? "

" Well, you've tried it before, haven't you? "

" Never seriously. I'm serious now. I've smoked my last cigarette."

She shook her head. " It won't work. For one thing, when you don't smoke, you can't write."

" Of course I can write without smoking. What I can't do is write when I'm worried and upset. Look at me now—I ought to be upstairs working, but what would be the use? Every nerve I've got is screaming. But it's all my own fault, I see that, and it's up to me now to put it right. I'm going to turn that man out and then we're going to start saving money."

Meg stood upright among the rosebushes.

" Marcus, d'you think we *can* turn him out? "

" Leave it to me," he said.

" I mean, there's a legal side to it. Perhaps he's got a right to stay."

" No one could have a right to stay who behaved like he did last night."

" I'm not at all sure about that. And then—perhaps we oughtn't to try to get rid of him until we know what's happened to Daphne."

Marcus's fingers clawed at a cigarette. He had one half-out of the packet before he stopped himself. He gave his hand a puzzled look, rather as if he wondered whom it belonged to, then he locked both hands together behind him and started stamping up and down again.

" Leave it to me," he muttered. " Just leave it to me, There are more ways than one of approaching the problem. Any problem."

But unfortunately for Marcus, he found it very difficult, unless his thoughts were being put straight down on to paper, to go on thinking constructively about any subject for more than a very short while. His moods were tenacious but his mind had a way of wandering. So in a few minutes' time he had ceased to think about how to turn Gerald Chilby out of the cottage and had gone back to brooding on his own failings.

Realising presently that this had happened, he was filled suddenly with the need for action, immediate blind unconsidered action. Turning in his tracks as if he had just heard someone shouting his name, he went running out into the road, wheeled into the garden next door, and pounded up the path to the cottage.

Meg saw him go, gave a sigh and snipped off far more than she had intended of their Betty Uprichard.

About a quarter of an hour later Marcus returned.

He came in thoughtfully, sat down in front of the sitting-room fire and lit a cigarette. Kate had come back from the Priory and Meg had come in from the garden to make tea. Marcus remained silent, smoking and glowering at the fire until she brought in the tea-tray, then he gulped two cups of tea, went up to his room and started to hammer his typewriter.

He was not working on his novel. He was writing a letter to his solicitor, asking him how to get rid of a tenant who refused to go.

Marcus was still unusually silent when he, Meg and Kate set off later to have dinner with Miss Harbottle. He remained so silent throughout the evening that Meg grew restive and after a while apologised for his behaviour to the old lady.

Miss Harbottle said that she had noticed that something was amiss and that she hoped he had no serious worry on his mind. Less obviously than Marcus, she herself was preoccupied.

" It's this trouble of poor Mr. Cronan's," she said. " I saw him this afternoon and he's in a shocking state. He'd still no news of his wife. In his shoes I believe I should not be excessively worried, but I know quite well my heart is a rather stony one. If someone I disliked as much as I'm sure he must dislike that woman were to disappear suddenly, I should celebrate. All the same, I wonder what *has* happened to her."

" Whatever it is," Marcus said, " that man Chilby's responsible for it. I don't know what connection there may be between the two of them, but the fact that the last that seems to have been seen of her was in his cottage —*our* cottage—seems to me to have a significance that can't be overlooked."

" That sounds to me as if you're suggesting that he's murdered her," Miss Harbottle said, " but even to me, that seems to be going rather far, unless you've some evidence of it."

" I have evidence," Marcus said.

Meg's knife slipped on her plate and she sent a piece of mutton shooting off it on to the polished mahogany of the table.

" Oh dear," she said miserably, " oh dear, he shouldn't say things like that, should he, Miss Harbottle? "

" Perhaps he means it," Miss Harbottle said. " Do you, Marcus? "

" My evidence is, I admit, rather subjective," Marcus said. " What it consists of is the fact that when I went to see Chilby this afternoon, breathing fire and slaughter, he took about two minutes to scare the wits out of me. And I still haven't got them back."

" You haven't," Meg said.

" And I don't know exactly how he did it, either," Marcus said. " He didn't threaten me, he didn't use violence. He simply gave me a feeling of . . ." He frowned into space. "I've been trying ever since to decide just what the feeling was."

"But did he say anything about Mrs. Cronan?" Miss Harbottle asked.

"It was a feeling. . . . About Daphne, did you say? No, I don't think so. A feeling of . . . Well, were you ever, as a child, frightened of the dark, or of rooms that seemed to be empty, and yet, when you went into them, gave you an immediate sense that there was evil there?"

"Not only as a child," Miss Harbottle said. "I've been frightened of ghosts all my life, but somehow I've managed to learn to live with them."

"I don't mean ghosts," Marcus said. "I mean evil—living evil. It's a thing with which I've had surprisingly little direct contact. I've known very few deliberately cruel or even seriously dishonest people. Even in the war I was fortunate enough to see very little human bestiality at really close quarters. So when I come face to face with it, I feel mainly a sort of childish inexperience. I think that's perhaps what really frightened me—my own ignorance and inexperience."

"I've often said you insist on leading a much too sheltered life," Meg said. "But none of this means that that man murdered Daphne."

"He's murdered somebody," Marcus said.

"I've always believed," Miss Harbottle said, "that the brand of Cain was quite invisible to the naked eye."

"He's murdered somebody, or else he's going to," Marcus said.

"Plain unpleasantness now," Miss Harbottle went on, "can take the risk of being recognised. Society is so tolerant. The most incredibly unpleasant and unsatisfactory people survive into middle life, or even old age, without getting into serious trouble, except sometimes with their nearer relations. And they, of course, are usually equally unpleasant. But the sort of evil that you're talking about, Marcus, has to disguise itself very skilfully in order to get beyond early youth."

" I don't believe there's such a thing as *evil* in early youth," Meg said.

" You don't believe there's such a thing at all," Marcus said. " That's why Chilby imposed on you so easily."

" In my view, which is frankly old-fashioned," Miss Harbottle said, " early youth is an almost entirely evil period, and it's only if people are very very kind and clever with one that one is sometimes successfully tamed. I can remember, in my own childhood, being savage, destructive, envious and dishonest. As to the taming process . . ."

The telephone rang.

Miss Harbottle excused herself and went out to answer it.

A moment after she had gone, Kate said, " That almost sounds as if she were trying to tell us that she's capable of murder herself. I wonder if she is."

" Of course she is," Marcus said. " So are you. So am I."

" No," Meg said. " I don't believe it. And I don't believe you were really frightened of Chilby at all. If anything frightened you, it was just the state you'd worked yourself up into, saying all of a sudden you were going to stop smoking and so on—just as it probably was in those empty rooms of your childhood."

" I *am* going to stop smoking," he said.

" I don't believe that either."

" I tell you, I've smoked my last cigarette."

" You told me that this afternoon."

" That was different. I'd had a shock. But now I'm prepared. I know what I'm up against. And I've got to stop smoking, it's the only solution." He gazed dourly at a baked potato on his plate. " When I make my mind up to a thing, I can do it," he said.

The door opened and Miss Harbottle came in again.

From her face it was plain that something was seriously

wrong. She stood still in the doorway, while Maggie, who had immediately sensed that trouble had come to them, appeared at her elbow.

"There's some very bad news, I'm afraid," Miss Harbottle said. "That was Richard Velden. They've found poor Mrs. Cronan. They found her in the river, just below Elsie Wibley's cottage. Mr. Cronan's at the Priory now with Richard. He asked—Richard asked—if you would go there, Marcus. I think he needs help with Mr. Cronan, and you're a friend of his."

Marcus had risen. "Of course. Did he tell you . . .?"

"How she died?" After a very slight pause, Miss Harbottle shook her head. "He just asked for you. I told him I was sure you would go at once."

Marcus's eyes met Meg's for an instant, then he went out.

Meg and Kate had also risen to their feet. Maggie came farther into the room. The four women stood there in silence, each except Kate taking a swift look into the faces of the other three, then, with a kind of awkwardness, turning away, as if they felt that those looks had betrayed to the others a thought that should have remained private.

Kate looked only at Miss Harbottle and went on looking at her.

"He did tell you something more, didn't he?" she said.

The old lady's face had become bleak and remote.

"He sounded very excited and upset," she said. "I think that we should wait to hear what Marcus has to tell us."

"But he did tell you——"

"No," Miss Harbottle said sharply.

"It would be best, wouldn't it," Meg said, "if Kate and I went home now?"

"Is that what you'd prefer? Perhaps—yes, perhaps that would be best," Miss Harbottle said.

" Kate——" Meg began.

Maggie interrupted, " Mr. Jeacock took the car. I heard it."

" Yes, of course," Miss Harbottle said. " But I can drive you home, if you wish, Margaret."

" Oh, ma'am, it's cold out this evening," Maggie said agitatedly. " You didn't ought to go out."

" That's all right, Maggie. I think Mrs. Jeacock's quite right, it would be best to go home. Mr. Jeacock will expect that, and return there himself."

" I hadn't thought of the car," Meg said.

There were tears in Maggie's eyes, tears that must have sprung from the thought of death in itself, or else, since they could scarcely have come from grief for Daphne Cronan, whom she had barely known, from some private source of distress or anxiety.

" Perhaps it would be better to stay," Meg said uneasily.

But she wanted to take Kate home. She wanted to take her as quickly as she could beyond the range of the understanding scrutiny of the two old women.

Here she was judging Kate by herself. To have her thoughts and feelings read by others, when she did not intend to reveal them, was to Meg dreadful, and there was about Kate's face at that moment a nakedness that made Meg feel the same sort of terror for her as she would have felt on her own account.

That Kate might not mind having her thoughts read, that there might even at last be relief in it, that she might in fact be seeking it, as she stood looking straight at Miss Harbottle, was a possibility that did not even occur to Meg. To get Kate home, to give her time to adjust some disguise of the emotion that blazed so blatantly in her pale face, seemed to Meg her first responsibility.

It was not until later that Meg began to ask herself what the emotion had been and to wonder what Miss Harbottle had made of it. She showed as little recognition of it as she could, turning away from it to look with concern at Maggie.

" I shan't be gone long, Maggie," she said. " You don't mind being left alone for a little while, do you? "

Maggie's tear-filled frightened eyes showed that she did, but she shook her head.

" Only you didn't ought to go out when it's so cold," she mumbled. " Mrs. Jeacock, you won't let her stay out long, will you? "

" I shan't be long," Miss Harbottle repeated.

She drove Meg and Kate home in her ancient, once noble car, saying very little and driving faster than she usually did, as if she were truly anxious to return to Maggie as quickly as possible.

As they came in sight of the Jeacocks' house, seeing a light there, she exclaimed, " Look—no, surely that can't be Marcus already! "

" No, that's Mr. Chilby, our tenant," Meg explained.

" When Marcus does come back," Miss Harbottle said, stopping the car by the gate, " perhaps you'd ask him to telephone me."

Meg thought that Marcus would probably telephone Miss Harbottle, or return to her house, before he came home, but she did not say so.

" Of course," she said. " You really won't come in? "

Miss Harbottle shook her head. " After all these years, Maggie's still terrified of being alone in that house at night, and she's terrified when I take the car out in the dark. And she's terrified of death—though not, I think, much of her own. Katherine——"

Kate had just got out of the car. She was standing in the road, gazing away into the shadows with a lost, dreaming expression on her face. She seemed quite unconscious now of the presence of anyone near her.

" Katherine, how much longer are you remaining——? " Miss Harbottle began, but then, looking at Kate, changed her mind. " Remember to ring me up," she said to Meg in a low voice as she re-started the car.

" And when you get her inside, I'd give her some brandy."

Meg nodded and as Miss Harbottle began the awkward job of reversing the big car in the narrow lane, slipped her arm through Kate's and drew her towards the house.

In the sitting-room, the fire had burnt low. Meg poked it, added some wood to it, and kneeling on the hearth, began blowing with the bellows at the small glow that remained.

Kate stood in the middle of the room, watching her.

After a moment Meg said to her, " If you'll do this for me, I'll get the brandy."

Kate knelt beside her, taking the bellows from her.

" What didn't she want to tell us? " she asked. " There was something, wasn't there? "

" Was there? " Meg said.

" Something about the way that Daphne died."

" I don't know."

" Didn't you notice how she looked when Marcus asked her that? "

" Not specially."

Meg went towards the door.

" He did," Kate said. " He knew she was warning him not to go on asking her questions."

" I didn't notice," Meg said and went out.

She went first to the kitchen, put coffee and water into the percolator and set it on the stove. Then she went to the dining-room and fetched glasses and a bottle of brandy from a cupboard in the sideboard.

When she returned to the sitting-room, Kate was still kneeling in front of the fireplace, still pointing the bellows at the faint red glow amongst the ashes, but forgetting to work them.

" You did, of course," she said, as if there had been no interruption. " And I need to talk about it much more than I need brandy. There are all kinds of things I need to talk about."

" Well then, I did notice it," Meg said, " but I don't know what it meant."

She poured out a little brandy for each of them, took the bellows from Kate and started working them fiercely.

"Richard told her something when he telephoned," Kate went on, "that she didn't want to tell us. Or she didn't want to tell you in front of me. I think I know what it was. It's that Daphne committed suicide or was murdered."

" *Murdered?* " Meg said shrilly.

"That's what I think," Kate said.

Meg shuddered. As much as anything, it was the calm of Kate's voice that sent the prickle up Meg's spine. At the same time, it made her wonder if Kate knew what she was saying.

Meg had thought of murder herself. She had thought of it the moment Daphne's death had been mentioned, thought of it and dismissed it as a nightmare fantasy. But Kate, in the quiet that had looked like stupor, had been thinking about it, so it now appeared, quite seriously.

Shrinking from this realisation, Meg said, "What are those other things you need to talk about?"

"You don't want me to," Kate said.

"I don't know. I don't know what they are."

As Meg worked the bellows, a small flame began to creep up round one of the logs that she had laid on the hearth.

"I think you've had more of a shock than you realise and you may say things you'll regret later on," she said. "We're very old friends and that means—that means you have to be very careful what you say. It's awful to say too much to anyone you're intimate with."

"What are you afraid I'll tell you?" Kate asked. "What was Miss Harbottle afraid that I'd say? That I think Roger murdered Daphne?"

The bellows seemed to take a leap in Meg's hands and dropped with a clatter on to the bricks. She looked at them in dismay, as if they had hurt her. Then she stood up and hurried out to the kitchen to look after the coffee.

She was putting the percolator and some cups on a

tray when she heard Kate leave the sitting-room and go upstairs. Meg waited uncertainly for a moment, then she followed her, calling to her as she went, " Kate—Kate, I'm such a fool. Don't take any notice of me. I've had a shock too and I'm scared."

Kate, ahead of her, paused at her bedroom door. She turned to face her.

" But suppose that is what I was going to tell you? " she said.

" Say it then, if you want to," Meg said. " Say what you like."

" So that you can tell me I'm wrong? "

" I shan't tell you anything. I shouldn't know what to tell you."

Kate opened her bedroom door. " No, and when I think about it, I don't really know what I want to say to you. A minute or two ago I thought I did—things about Roger, about Aunt Chris and the way *she* died— Oh! " The exclamation came sharply as she turned to go into her room.

It brought Meg quickly to her side. They stood together in the doorway, looking across the bedroom at the window.

It was open and the light was on in Gerald Chilby's room. A reflection of his room should have shone at them across the dark space between window and doorway. Yet all that they could see was the night sky, glittering with stars.

Kate crossed to the window. She fingered the jagged edges of glass that still clung to the frame and said wonderingly, " He's broken it."

# CHAPTER XI

MEG'S FIRST RESPONSE to the discovery was violent anger. After the mounting strain of the last few days, the broken window seemed the last straw.

Also, without her quite realising the fact, it was a welcome distraction. To rush straight round to the cottage, to hammer on the door, to demand explanations with fury and much shouting, to behave, in other words, as Marcus would probably have behaved in the circumstances, appeared extremely attractive.

But several things prevented this. The main thing was Meg's own nature. She sometimes thought that she wanted to make scenes, but except very occasionally and in the greatest privacy, she rarely trusted herself to carry the scene through with sufficient style.

Besides this, as soon as she had given herself time to think a little, she recognised that to fuss about a broken window while she and Kate were waiting for further news of Daphne Cronan's death, would suggest the loss of all sense of proportion. The fuss, indeed, would soon, in her own mind, come to seem indecent. Another thing that worked on Meg almost immediately was the look on Kate's face.

The look was puzzled, thoughtful and calculating.

With one of her long, thin fingers still lightly touching one of the sharp points of glass that stuck out from the window-frame, Kate turned her head and stared at the lighted window of the cottage.

" But *why*? " she said softly.

Meg looked at Gerald Chilby's window.

Looking at it directly, she could see far less of the room than she would have been able to see mirrored in Kate's window-pane. A patch of cream-painted wall and white ceiling, a corner of the second window in the room and the unshaded electric light bulb, dangling at the end of a few inches of flex, was all that came within her field of vision.

" He was afraid we'd spy on him," Meg said. " The horrible man! "

" To stop that, it would have been much more sensible to hang up a curtain," Kate said.

" I don't suppose he's got any curtains."

" Then he could have pinned up a blanket or something. After all, if we really want to, we can still spy on him. All we've got to do is hold a mirror out of the window."

" Perhaps he doesn't believe we'll go as far as that."

" I'd say he was the sort of man who'd believe the worst of everyone."

" Then he just wasn't clever enough to think of a mirror. Or else—or else he just did it to annoy us and insult us." Meg was puzzled by Kate's concentration on the problem. " Let's go downstairs again," she said. " The coffee's ready."

She crossed the dark bedroom to the doorway and switched on the light.

Turning away from the window, Kate took off her coat and dropped it on the bed.

" D'you think it's possible, Meg, that that man's a policeman? " she asked.

A rather wild look came into Meg's brown eyes.

" No," she said flatly. " Marcus was quite right about him. He's a crook of some sort."

" A private detective, then," Kate said. " The kind who might go in for blackmail."

" I don't know, I really don't know. Let's go downstairs again and have some coffee."

" It's because of those questions he asked about Aunt Chris and the way she died," Kate said. But she followed Meg to the door and along the passage. " He was hinting, wasn't he, that she was murdered? And if you think about it, perhaps it's strange that no one else ever hinted at it. Or did they, I wonder."

" Kate! " Meg said in a horrified tone. " Don't—*don't* say things like that! You can do terrible harm—I'm sure you can—by simply saying them."

" I wonder," Kate repeated.

But in the sitting-room, beside the fire, which was crackling now and beginning to warm the room, and with the coffee-tray between them, Kate, to Meg's relief, did not pursue this subject.

Instead she became silent, and when Meg spoke to her, only regarded her vacantly, as if she had not heard her.

Meg gulped the hot coffee eagerly and pouring herself out a second cup, wondered what Kate was really thinking about. Was it the death of Daphne Cronan and the fact that it had set Roger Cronan free to marry her, or was it still of the death of Miss Velden? Or was she thinking of something quite different?

Kate was sitting crouched in her chair, nursing her cup in both her thin long hands. Her fair hair flopped forward round her face. Her eyes were lowered. She looked fragile, vague and withdrawn, with that air she so often had of having no connection with the place in which she happened to find herself.

Meg grew more and more anxious for Marcus's return. When at last he came he was not alone. She heard him speaking to someone as he came through the garden to the house. Though she did not hear any answer, she guessed that it was Roger.

She was startled when he brought Richard Velden into the room.

She saw that Kate was startled too, but after the first blankness of surprise, there was relief in her eyes, or so Meg thought.

Marcus pounced at once on the bottle of brandy, then looked around desperately for glasses, as if their absence were an important link in the chain of calamity.

Meg fetched them and Marcus poured out two stiff drinks.

Handing one to Richard, he said to Meg and Kate, " There's a lot to tell you and it's all of it bad. As bad as could be."

" Where's Roger? " Meg asked.

Kate said nothing.

" Gone back into Carringdon," Marcus said. " He wouldn't come with us. I tried to get him to come here for the night, but it wasn't any good. I've got to tell you—I may as well get it over quickly—that Daphne's death is probably murder. There's a possibility of suicide, but accident is out. She was shot."

A tremor shook Kate's body as she crouched in the chair by the fire, but otherwise she did not stir. Her eyes were on Richard.

He was standing in the middle of the room. The hand that was holding the glass of brandy was not quite steady. His pale face had a bluish look, his clothes were splashed with mud and up to his knees his trousers were sodden.

Marcus went on, " Velden found her. . . . Get closer to the fire, Velden. You look frozen to the bone."

" I'm all right," Richard said, " and I'm just going. I just wanted to see how . . ." His eyes met Kate's at that point and he did not finish.

She said, " That's what you told Miss Harbottle, isn't it?—that it was murder or suicide."

" Yes," he said.

She stood up suddenly, stiff and straight.

" Will you all stop trying to protect me! Roger and I are in love—yes! And now Roger's wife is dead and more than any of the rest of you I need to know the truth about it. Tell me what happened."

" Will you tell her, Velden? " Marcus asked. " Anyway, the first part of it."

" All right." Richard moved up to the fire, holding one foot close to it as he began to speak, looking down at the steam that mounted from the wet cloth and the soaked shoe.

" I went down to the cottage to speak to Elsie Wibley, as I promised you, Kate," he said. " I told her she needn't leave the cottage. She talked and talked. . . . I don't know how long I was there—about three-quarters of an hour, I think. When I came out I thought I'd drop in on Thea Arkwright before going home. The shortest way to her bungalow from the cottage is across the river by the ferry. It was over the other side. I started turning the crank and the ferry started coming over. But there seemed to be something wrong with it. It—it seemed to keep sticking. And then I saw . . ." His voice dried up in his throat. He drank some brandy and started coughing.

" She'd got caught underneath it somehow, I don't know how," he went on. " As soon as I saw her I waded in. I don't mean I could see then who she was, but I could see it was a woman. I got her on to the bank before I really saw who she was. I got Elsie then. I told her to go and telephone for Cronan, but she got hysterical —said she couldn't telephone, she was too deaf. So I got across on the ferry and went to Thea's and got her to telephone to Cronan and the police, then I went back and waited. They—they seemed an age getting there— the police, I mean, but they got there first. They found Daphne's car in the bushes a little way below the ferry. They also found—what I suppose I might have found if I'd looked, that . . ." His voice cracked again. He gave a swift look at Marcus.

Marcus went on, " They found that Daphne hadn't died by drowning, but from a shot through the head. That's to say, there'll be a post-mortem, but actually there's no doubt of it. And it must have happened something like twenty-four hours before they found her, and it could—it just could have been suicide, but they haven't found the gun yet."

" And Roger? " Kate said.

" He came," Richard said, " and I took him back to the Priory, as soon as the police would let me. He was very quiet, said hardly anything, wouldn't answer questions. They—the police—came and started firing questions at him and he wouldn't answer any of them. It was then I telephoned for Jeacock. I thought Cronan was doing the worst thing for himself that he could and I thought Jeacock might be able to reason with him. I remembered your telling me you were all going to Miss Harbottle's for dinner, so I rang there." He drank the rest of his brandy and set the glass down. " That's all."

" Except," Marcus said, " that the police will be round here soon, Kate, to ask you about your meeting with Daphne last night." In a grimmer tone he added, " And to speak to Mr. Chilby."

Richard bent towards Kate and laid a hand on her shoulder. As if the touch of his hand were cold, she gave a shiver.

" Don't look like that, Kate—he didn't do it," he said softly. Then he turned towards the door. " I'll get home now."

" Chilby! " Meg exclaimed. " The window! "

It halted Richard. He looked at her questioningly.

" He broke his window—our window—I mean, Kate's window," she said. Pressing both hands to her head, she tried to clear the fog of horror from her mind. " But I don't suppose it has anything to do with it. It couldn't have. I mean, if Daphne was killed yesterday evening, Chilby's breaking Kate's window this evening is just— just something else. Not anything important."

Richard turned with raised eyebrows to Marcus.

" I think we'll take a look at this window," Marcus said.

But he did not go upstairs to Kate's bedroom. He went into the garden and stood below the window, looking up at it. Richard and Meg followed him.

Kate stayed where she was, standing in front of the fire.

But as soon as she was alone she gave a long moan, a sound almost like a suppressed scream, and buried her face in her hands.

From the lawn below the window the broken window-pane showed plainly as an oblong of darkness instead of one that faintly reflected the starlight.

" I don't understand," Richard said. " What did he do it for? "

Meg explained how the window-pane had reflected the interior of the cottage.

Marcus had stooped. He was feeling about on the grass and after a moment said, " Yes, here's a piece of it." He held up a piece of broken glass. " He must have thrown something at the window, or poked at it with a long stick—a broom-handle or something."

" Must be crazy—crazier than I thought," Richard muttered.

" You do know him then? " Marcus said.

" He came to see me to-day."

" That's all? "

" That's all."

Marcus started walking fast towards the gate.

Meg called after him, " For heaven's sake, where are you going? "

" To speak to Chilby," he answered over his shoulder.

" But not now! "

" Yes, now."

" But the window doesn't really matter."

" Chilby does, though."

Meg looked at Richard, making a helpless gesture with her hands. " I wish I hadn't mentioned it."

" Oh, I don't know," he said. " Could be, at a time like this, that it's best to look into anything that's out of the ordinary. But I'll be going now. If there's anything I can do, I'll be at home."

" Thank you," she answered.

They could both hear Marcus pounding on the door of the cottage.

"And take care of Kate," Richard said. "I've an idea she's going to need it."

He walked off quickly.

Meg stood looking after him. She almost called him back to ask him what he had meant, because Meg herself could imagine several quite different things from which Kate might need protection, little as Kate might be prepared to accept it. But as Richard's slim figure disappeared into the shadows, Meg turned back into the house.

A minute or two later Marcus reappeared.

"Seems not to be in," he said.

"But his light's on," Meg said.

"Then he's decided not to answer the door."

"Well, it doesn't matter. To-morrow will do——" She broke off as Kate, without any word of what she meant to do, moved suddenly to the door. "Where are you going?" Meg asked.

"I'm going to look into Chilby's room," Kate said. "I want to see what we're not meant to see."

"But you can't——" Meg began.

"I'll use a mirror."

"I meant, you can't just deliberately look into his room."

"Scruples," Marcus said, "at a time like this! Whatever next? Kate's quite right. Let's all go."

He followed her out.

Reluctantly and with her small face puckered with distress, Meg followed him. They went upstairs together and without turning on the light, went into Kate's room.

There was a hand-mirror on the dressing-table. Kate picked it up and was going to the window with it when Marcus took it from her. She did not protest, but stood beside Meg, waiting, while Marcus held the mirror out of the window, moving it about uncertainly until he found the angle at which it reflected best the inside of the cottage bedroom.

Kate and Meg knew when he had found it because of

his sudden rigidity. Then he withdrew the mirror. He turned to face them.

"It looks to me," he said, "as if our tenant has managed to get himself murdered too."

# CHAPTER XII

IT WAS AT about nine o'clock the next morning that Detective-Inspector Wylie, accompanied by Sergeant Wall, paid a visit to the Cronans' house in Carringdon.

The house overlooked the square in the centre of the town. It was a narrow-fronted three-storied house in an attractive Georgian terrace. Roger's offices occupied the ground floor. On the floor above there was one big room, which could be divided in two by folding doors, and a small kitchen.

When the bell rang, Roger, in his dressing-gown, was in the kitchen, making coffee. There was no one in the office, because Roger had telephoned his assistants, telling them not to come.

He did not know how many pots of coffee he had made during the night. At some time, perhaps about two o'clock in the morning, he had got undressed and gone to bed, but that had not been a success and he had soon got up again.

Some hours later he had had a bath and shaved. Early in the night he had finished what had been left in the whisky bottle and with apprehension had watched the dwindling of his stock of cigarettes, wondering if he could possibly make them last till the shop on the corner opened. Then in one of Daphne's handbags he had found a packet of the filter-tipped kind that she liked to smoke.

He was smoking almost the last of these and was making up his mind to get into some clothes and go down to the shop when he heard the door-bell ring.

At the sound he suddenly became dizzy. The little

kitchen, with heaps of drying coffee-grounds spilled over the sink and draining-boards, swam round him. He clutched the edge of the sink, leaning against it, his eyes closed, a feeling of sickness in his throat. There was a pounding in his head. He did not believe that he would be able to get down the stairs.

But after a moment he felt steadier. He turned to the door, letting his cigarette drop to the floor and treading it out.

As the bell rang a second time, he started down the stairs. Although it had been daylight for several hours, the lights were still on on the landing and staircase, but he did not notice this.

He had guessed it was the police who had called and he recognised Inspector Wylie as the man who had questioned him at length the evening before. This was a relief to Roger, not because he had taken any special liking to Wylie, a solid quiet and deliberate man, who looked as if his thoughts were occupied with a private worry about some internal pain. But Roger had not disliked him either and at least with him there would be no need to go over all the same ground again.

Not that Roger had stopped going over it for more than a few minutes at a time throughout the night. The things that Daphne had said and done during the last few days, and the things that he himself had said and done, particularly the things that he had said and done between the times when he had left Kate at the Jeacocks' house on the Sunday morning and when, on the evening of the same day, he had first telephoned the police to tell them that his wife was missing, had gone round and round endlessly in his mind until he had begun to feel that he would never again be free to think of anything else.

He took Wylie and the sergeant up to the sitting-room. Here also the lights were still on. The curtains were drawn and the air was stale with smoke.

Drawing back the curtains, Roger opened a window.

The morning was cloudy and there was a damp chill in the air that penetrated his exhausted body. He saw that it must have rained in the night, for the street and the pavements were wet.

"Please go ahead with your breakfast, if we've interrupted you," Wylie said.

"I was just making some coffee," Roger answered.

"Just coffee? How long is it, then, since you've eaten, Mr. Cronan?"

"I'm not sure." So far as Roger could remember, he had not eaten since midday the day before.

"You'd better eat," Wylie said. "Putting it off is one of the things that does you no good."

"I'll have something presently," Roger said. "May I ask what's brought you now? Is it any—any special thing?"

"Then you haven't heard from Mr. Jeacock this morning?"

"No." Roger's voice had gone hoarse. "What's happened? What is it?"

"The man Chilby," Wylie said, "who rented the cottage that belongs to Mr. and Mrs. Jeacock, was found dead there last night."

"Chilby—the man my wife went to see?"

"Yes."

Roger looked at him vacantly.

"According to the medical evidence," Wylie went on, "it happened probably between about seven o'clock and eight-thirty last night."

"How?" Roger croaked, his voice still out of control.

"He was shot—possibly with the same weapon that killed your wife, though we haven't corroboration of this yet. It was there on the floor beside him."

Roger groped for a chair and dropped into it. The feeling of dizziness had come back, this time with a sense that there was something pleasant about it, that in letting the room and the two faces before him sway and then swirl away from him into a grey distance he was promised a wonderful release.

But he knew that it was still too soon to let the feeling overcome him.

Holding his head in his hands, he said, " Do you mean that he murdered her and then killed himself? "

" No," Wylie said.

" But if the gun—No." Roger stopped himself. One didn't argue with a man like Wylie. One listened, waited and tried to understand. That was what Wylie did himself. Listened, waited, watched and went on thinking about that pain inside him. What was it? A gastric ulcer, perhaps.

Wylie waited now for a moment, then said, " Your wife's wound, just possibly, could have been self-inflicted. It isn't likely, because to go down to the river, drive her car into the bushes, then get on to that ferry or else wade a little way out into the water and then shoot herself, is an almost too fantastic way of committing suicide. Still, fantastic suicides do happen. But Chilby was shot from the doorway of the room, when he was standing near the window."

" By the same person who murdered my wife? "

" I can't tell you that yet. And unfortunately we haven't been able to find anyone who heard either shot, and I don't suppose we shall be able to. Miss Wibley, who might have heard the one, if she was at home, is very deaf, and the Jeacocks' house was empty. And both spots are pretty solitary."

Roger had lifted his head and was returning Wylie's gaze. " Who was this man Chilby? "

" I was hoping you might be able to tell me something about him," Wylie said.

" I can't."

" Yet you know your wife went to see him on the day she died? "

" So the Jeacocks told me. That is, as I understood it, she didn't go to see him, she went to look for something in the cottage. When Miss Hawthorne saw her reflection in the window, she appeared to be searching for something, having watched the place, I suppose, until she knew that Chilby had gone out."

" That's at least how Miss Hawthorne described it."

" Do you mean you don't believe her? "

Wylie moved his heavy shoulders in a very faint shrug.

Roger said sharply, " She'd no reason to lie about it."

" None that I know of," Wylie said. " It's rather early to decide yet what I do or don't believe. I'd hoped you could help me."

" By giving you some information about Chilby? "

" Yes."

" I never saw him in my life. I never heard of him until Marcus Jeacock told me they'd let the cottage to him—and I don't think I even heard his name then. Jeacock just told me on the telephone that they'd let the cottage."

" You know that Chilby claimed she'd stolen something from his room? "

" I thought he accused Miss Hawthorne."

" I'm sorry—yes, you're right. And Miss Hawthorne said nothing then about having seen Mrs. Cronan in the cottage, but later told Mr. and Mrs. Jeacock that she had."

Roger nodded. A spark of anger in his tired eyes had brought a little life into his face. " I believe so."

" Yet you can offer no suggestion of any kind as to what your wife might have been looking for."

" Listen," Roger said, " I told you last night, I made no secret of it, my wife and I hadn't been on good terms for a long time. She'd left me once and I'd started divorce proceedings. Then she came back and I—I let her stay. Later I regretted it. I was in love with Miss Hawthorne, I still am, I'd been hoping . . ." Again he checked himself, feeling that he was playing straight into Wylie's hands.

Don't argue, he told himself. Listen, wait, try to understand.

Wylie's grave, aloof face showed little interest in what Roger had said, but he asked, " Is it possible that Chilby was someone whom your wife met during her absence? "

" Of course it's possible," Roger said. " But he wasn't the man for whom she left me, if that's what you're going to suggest. I told you last night who he was, I gave you his address. And I don't believe Chilby was another lover. I don't know if I can make you understand this, but Daphne wasn't secretive about such things. In fact, rather the reverse."

Wylie nodded. " I wasn't thinking of him in that relation. There are other possibilities. He might, for instance, have been blackmailing her, or somebody she knew. She might even have been helping him in this. There are all kinds of theories that could more or less fit the facts. But until we know more than we do at present about the man himself, it wouldn't help much to commit ourselves to any of them. At present all we know about him is the name he gave to the Jeacocks, which may or may not have been his real one, that he claimed to have spent most of his life abroad, that he visited Mr. Velden yesterday morning, that, according to Mr. Velden, he offered to buy Shandon Priory for a sum which Mr. Velden considered ridiculously low, and that he kept a small diary—no, not a diary, an appointment book, in which there were a few jottings. Most of them don't mean anything to us yet, but there's one that's certainly important. It was for Sunday evening. That's the day before he was killed. It said, ' 7.30—D.V.' "

" ' D.V.' . . . Deo volente? " Roger said. " Something was to happen at seven-thirty—D.V."

" Could be. There's another thing. He'd brought a gun with him to East Shandon, or so Miss Hawthorne says. She says she saw him, in that reflection in her window, which I dare say she told you about, holding what she believes was a gun. But someone last night broke that window. Not by shooting at it, by the way —no signs of a bullet. That's all very interesting. And there's still another interesting fact we've discovered since last night. We've found out where your wife went immediately after leaving Chilby's cottage."

That brought Roger's head up quickly. His muscles went rigid.

" Where? "

" To see Mrs. Arkwright."

Roger's eyes clouded with bewilderment. Then he said thoughtfully, " Yesterday at the Jeacocks'—I thought —yes, I remember I thought she knew something. She was there and she got up in a hurry and said she'd got to go off to some meeting or other and somehow I got the feeling that it was because she didn't want to tell me something."

" She didn't volunteer the information," Wylie said dryly. " Some children saw your wife's car at her gate. We questioned her about it and she admitted then that your wife had come to see her."

" And Daphne was found," Roger said dazedly, " in the river, close, quite close, to Thea Arkwright's bungalow."

" That's going a little too fast, Mr. Cronan," Wylie said.

" Yes," Roger agreed. " But what reason does Mrs. Arkwright give for my wife's visit to her? "

" No reason worth mentioning. Says she dropped in on her for a drink."

" She wouldn't have done that. Not, I mean, unless she had a purpose of some sort."

" They weren't very friendly? "

" Not at all."

Roger saw that this was not news to Wylie. So probably he also knew why Daphne and Thea had not been friends.

Roger began to think about Thea, to wonder about her. He had never thought much about her before. She was a friend of the Jeacocks', someone he occasionally met in the houses of other friends, someone with whom he would stand and chat for a few minutes if he happened to meet her in the streets of Carringdon. He had heard that she was supposed to be in love with Richard Velden.

Wylie gave him time to turn these thoughts over in his mind, then asked him, " If they weren't friends, would you go so far as to say they were enemies? "

Roger shook his head. Yet as he did so, he began to wonder how deep the antagonism between the two women might really have gone. The fact that he had never taken it seriously did not mean that it had not been serious. The time when he had thought deeply and anxiously about Daphne's true feelings had long since passed. " But if my wife visited Mrs. Arkwright," he said, " there was a reason for it."

" Mrs. Arkwright did tell us," Wylie said, " that Mrs. Cronan asked her a good many questions about Miss Hawthorne."

" I suppose she might have done that."

" You mean, that might have been a sufficient reason to take her to see Mrs. Arkwright? "

Roger felt that a trap had been set and that he had walked into it.

" But it doesn't tie up with my wife's visit to Chilby," he said.

" No," Wylie said, " not on the face of it. Well, I think that's all for the moment, Mr. Cronan."

With a glance at the sergeant, he went towards the door.

Roger stood up.

To his own surprise, he felt far calmer than he had before the visit of the two men. It crossed his mind that when they had gone he would cook himself some bacon and eggs. He went downstairs with them.

At the door, Wylie asked him one more question.

" Mr. Cronan, am I right that most of Mr. Velden's friends call him Richard? "

Roger gave him a puzzled glance. "Yes, I believe they do. . . . Oh!" He suddenly saw the point of the question. "You mean they don't call him Dick. Dick Velden."

"Exactly," Wylie said. " 7.30—D.V.—Dick Velden."

"But if that's what it meant," Roger said, "if that's what Chilby wrote in his diary, it follows, doesn't it, that he and Velden knew one another better than Velden's admitted."

"I wondered if that's what you'd think," Wylie said as he and the sergeant went out into the street.

Roger closed the door after them. Then he went upstairs again and into the kitchen. Since it had occurred to him a few minutes before that he was hungry, the pangs had grown in him until by now he felt that they were not to be endured for another moment.

In a nervous hurry, he fried several rashers of bacon and two eggs, made two slices of toast and sat down to eat them at the kitchen table. He ate about half of what was on his plate, then pushed it away from him.

He sat for some minutes with his elbows on the table, a blank look on his face. Then he got up, went up to his bedroom on the top floor of the house and dressed quickly.

About half an hour later he arrived at Thea Arkwright's bungalow.

She came to the door, wearing an old corduroy house-coat that showed the hem of the pink nylon nightdress under it. Her hair was uncombed and she had no make-up on her face. There was a nervous glitter in her eyes and there were smears of tiredness under them.

Looking at Roger expressionlessly, she said his name in an unsurprised voice and told him to come in.

The sitting-room was a small square room with a bay-window that overlooked the river. The furniture all looked as if it had been picked up cheaply in second-hand salerooms. The wallpaper showed the unfaded patches left by some earlier occupant's pictures. There were newspapers and magazines scattered about the room, but the only books were a few paper-back detective stories and a telephone directory.

Though Roger's mind did not focus on the scene, he was aware that it was not as he had expected. Thea's tailor-made clothes were always good and she had never seemed to be short of money. But what this room implied was either that her income was more limited than he had ever supposed, or that she was totally indifferent to her surroundings.

" I know why you've come," she said dully, pressing the switch of an electric fire with her foot, then dropping into a chair close to it and holding her hands out to the reddening bars. " I nearly came to see you. I nearly came last night, when I heard. . . . But I didn't know. . . ." She gave a shiver, staring down at her hands, then turned her head to look up at him. " I didn't know if you'd want to see anyone just then."

Standing still only just inside the door, Roger said, " She came here."

" Yes, she came here immediately after she'd been to see Chilby—or so she told me," Thea replied.

" She *told* you that? " Roger said.

Thea nodded.

" But you didn't tell the police that," he said.

" No."

" You told them she'd just dropped in on you for a drink—for no special reason."

" Yes."

" That wasn't true, then. There was a reason."

He came forward into the room. As he did so, she turned her head away. He stood near her, looking down at her ruffled, reddish hair.

" Why did she come, Thea? "

She put a hand over her eyes. " I've been trying to think what to say—to the police, I mean."

" Is it impossible to tell them the truth? "

" I don't know, I don't know! I've been trying to think. . . . I'll tell you about it, then perhaps you can tell me. . . . But I didn't see any sense in it at the time —I told her so—and I still don't. And there's been too much talk about it already, and if it doesn't really mean anything and it's only going to make trouble. . . ."

He frowned. Thea was usually all too emphatic in her speech, too clipped and definite. Listening to her now, a feeling came to him that in letting so many sentences fade out unfinished there must be something deliberate, or else that she had received some far greater shock than he had yet realised.

As if in answer to this last thought of his, she raised her eyes to his again and said, " You know I'm the last person who's known to have seen her alive, don't you? And it's known that we weren't friends."

" If you mean that you're under suspicion of her murder," Roger said, " so am I—far more so."

" Have they told you so—the police? "

" They don't need to put it in words."

" No," she agreed.

" Why *did* she come here, Thea? "

" Well, part of the difficulty in telling you about it is that she didn't put it quite into words herself," she said. " She talked a lot and quite strangely. She was very excited. She asked me a lot of things about Kate Hawthorne—I told the police about that. And she told me she'd been to see Chilby. What she didn't tell me was that she hadn't actually seen him, but had got into his cottage when he was with the Jeacocks. I only heard that from the police. That's to say, I don't think she told me in so many words that she'd seen him, though I can't remember for sure. I think she just let me think that she'd seen him and talked to him and that he'd told her this thing about Richard."

" What thing? "

" The thing she came to tell me about—I don't know why, unless it was just to hurt me, because she knew—

126

oh, everyone knows about it, so why shouldn't I say it?
—because she knew that I'm in love with him."

"What thing, Thea? What did she tell you about
him?"

"That he's a fake, an impostor. That this man we
know isn't Richard Velden at all."

She sprang to her feet, brushed past Roger and started
walking agitatedly up and down the small room.

"And it's so absurd, so impossible," she exclaimed,
thrusting a hand through her short hair, so that it stood
out wildly round her face. " *I* started that story, Roger.
It was all my own damn' fault, my own damn' stupidity.
And it didn't mean a thing. Of course it didn't. I'd
drunk too much and I was showing off, pretending I
knew a lot more about Richard than I really did. He's
a queer sort of chap and it's easy to have queer ideas
about him. If he's done some questionable things in his
time, it wouldn't surprise me at all. But how *could* he
be an impostor? I don't know how these things are done,
but I'm quite sure he'd have had to prove his identity
to a whole lot of lawyers before touching a penny of
Miss Velden's money. Isn't that so, Roger? Isn't an
impostor just about the one thing we can be quite sure
he isn't? Or am I wrong?" She stood still, fixing an
intense and questioning stare on his face. "Could I
possibly be wrong?"

He did not intend to be side-tracked. "Then Daphne
came here and told you that she had it from Chilby that
Velden—this man we've been calling Velden—is an
impostor. Is that what happened?"

"Yes. More or less. That's, anyway, how I understood
it." Thea started walking up and down again. "But she
didn't see Chilby, so he can't have told her that. She
must have found something in his room that made her
think it. And I think she came here straight afterwards
to—to make me suffer. That's the only thing I can think
of. Because—I don't have to pretend with you, do I?—
she was jealous of me. And perhaps she thought it was

just his money that I wanted. His money!" She made a queer sobbing noise, which sounded as if it might mount into hysterical laughter.

"But why did Daphne go to see Chilby at all?" The more excitement Thea showed, the calmer Roger became. It seemed to him that she was in a state of great fear for herself. He had not expected this and he thought it unreasonable, but in some way it lightened the cloud that had been on his mind, perhaps by reminding him that he was not the only person who might fear to be suspected of murder.

"Wasn't it that telephone call?" Thea said. "Didn't you hear about it? When we were all at the Priory on Saturday evening, a telephone call came for Richard which upset him badly. And immediately afterwards Daphne walked in. She'd been in the morning-room while he was speaking on the telephone and there's an extension in there. She could have listened and heard something that made her decide to go and talk to Chilby."

"Has Velden told you that that call was from Chilby?"

"I haven't seen him since that evening."

"You saw him last night."

She looked puzzled for an instant, then she said, "Oh, then. When he came here to get me to call the police. But we didn't talk then about anything but the finding of Daphne's body."

"No, I suppose not. So that's all guesswork—why she went to Chilby, I mean."

"Yes, it is really."

"And you haven't told any of this to the police?"

"Not yet. I'll have to, I suppose, but first—well, first I want to talk to Richard."

"To give him due warning, in case he's the murderer?"

"He isn't the murderer."

"Why not? If Chilby knew something about him and Daphne found it out, that gives Velden a motive for both murders."

" But he also happens to be able to prove where he was at the times when both murders happened."

" How do you know? "

" The police told me so."

" But alibis can sometimes be faked."

She stood still, again regarding him, but with a calmer gaze. " The fact is, you haven't any alibi at all, have you, Roger? And neither have I. And you had the best motive for Daphne's murder, and I had the best opportunity."

He nodded in agreement. " But Chilby's appearance in East Shandon had something to do with Velden, not with you or me."

She gave a bitter smile. " So you want to make Richard chief suspect, do you? I suppose that's natural, even though in your heart you must have been glad when you saw that Daphne was falling in love with him. But vanity dies hard, doesn't it? Only I don't think you should try to get a man hanged merely because he's hurt your vanity."

" I'm not trying yet to get anyone hanged." He went towards the door.

" Roger——"

He stopped.

She looked confused, as if for a moment she wondered why she had checked him. Then she said, " Could it be true—could it possibly be true—that Richard's a fake? "

" I don't know any more than you do," he answered. " I can only agree with you that it doesn't seem likely."

" No, it isn't likely, is it? " she said eagerly. " I know it isn't likely. And so there's no point in asking myself the question that's kept me awake all night—if he is a fake, what happened to the real Richard Velden? "

# CHAPTER XIII

THIS WAS A QUESTION to which Marcus Jeacock was fully convinced by now that he knew the answer.

He would not have claimed that his answer could have supplied any details as to what had happened to the real Richard Velden, though the image that hung before Marcus's mind's eye was complete in every particular. That dark quayside in Chicago, the black limousine, the hard-eyed sullen men, the shot, the splash, had all come as sharply into focus to his inner vision as if he were watching it all from a good seat in a cinema. But if someone had told him that there was evidence which showed that the murder had really happened in New York, or deep in the heart of the Perry Mason country, he would not have argued the point. It was merely that a certain conservatism in his imagination made him prefer Chicago as the background for the crime.

The point on which he would not have yielded was that among the faces of the killers, those of Gerald Chilby and of the man whom East Shandon had rather doubtingly accepted as Richard Velden, could be clearly recognised.

The rest was easy.

The false Richard Velden, equipped with proofs of his identity stolen from the dead man, had come to England and taken over Miss Velden's estate, then in some way had attempted to double-cross his associates. Gerald Chilby had followed him and on the telephone on Saturday evening had warned him that he need not expect to get away with it. Daphne Cronan, to her own misfortune, had eavesdropped on this conversation, had learnt the truth, or enough of it to guess at the rest, then had burgled Chilby's cottage, trying to find the proofs which would give her power over the man with whom she was, for the time being, violently in love.

With these proofs she had visited Thea Arkwright, to frighten her out of any further competition, then she had gone on to the Priory to challenge Velden with her knowledge. There, taking from her and using the gun that Daphne had just taken from Chilby's room, Velden had killed her and, repeating the pattern of the earlier crime, as Marcus believed was the foolish habit of criminals, had dumped her body in the river.

The next evening, having heard from Kate that she and the two Jeacocks would be spending the evening with Miss Harbottle, Velden—it was still easiest to call him that—had arranged to call on Chilby, had shot him and in a bungling attempt to make his death look like suicide, had thrown the gun down beside him. Then the thought had come to Velden that if he himself were now to discover Daphne's body, the act would help to direct suspicion away from him and to fix it on Chilby. Accordingly, he had made use of the pretext that Kate had given him to call on Elsie Wibley, and with her as an audience, had discovered both the body and the car.

There was only one serious difficulty about it all that Marcus could see. Inspector Wylie had told him that Richard Velden had impregnable alibis for both crimes. But this was not a difficulty that had much impressed Marcus. He was inclined to believe that the better the alibi, the greater the guilt.

This was what he said to Meg and Kate over a late breakfast, after giving them an outline of his suspicions, a very bare outline, shorn of all the colourful elaboration which was likely to make them laugh at him.

" Innocent people," he said, " just don't have alibis."

" They do," Meg said. " You've got one yourself."

" I haven't," he said. " How can I prove that when I left Miss Harbottle's house last night I didn't come straight back here and shoot Chilby before going to the Priory? And there's another thing—that entry in Chilby's diary. ' 7.30, D.V.' It's true we've all been calling this man Richard, not Dick, but if he and Chilby are really Americans, or at least if they've lived for a long time in America, it's quite certain they'd use the shortened version of his name. Anyway, it's highly probable."

" There's only one thing wrong with that," Meg said. " If Chilby and Richard knew each other well in America and if Richard's real name is, say Elmer D. Hackenbacker, why didn't Chilby write E.H. in his diary? "

" Caution," Marcus said. " The criminal's habitual caution."

Meg shook her head. " He didn't expect anyone but himself to see that diary. If Richard did these murders, which I don't believe, and then faked two alibis for himself, it wasn't because he isn't Richard Velden."

Kate raised her head. She had been sitting in a long silence while Marcus had talked, and he was not certain that she had been listening to him.

" He *is* Richard Velden," she said.

Marcus looked exasperated.

" All right then," he said, " I haven't got it all quite straight. Possibly Chilby's hold over him was that he knew that Richard had murdered Miss Velden, or something like that——"

" Something like that! " Meg cried. " Marcus, are you out of your mind? "

" Very nearly," he said through clenched teeth. " Very nearly." He stood up, looking at the window. In a quite different tone, he said, " Here's Roger."

He hurried out.

He met Roger half-way up the garden path, took him by the arm and started him walking up and down the lawn.

" Is Kate here? " Roger asked.

" Yes," Marcus said. " I tried to make her go back to London, but she wouldn't go. You've heard about Chilby? "

" Yes. I had a visit from the police this morning. Marcus, what does Kate think? "

" How does one ever know what Kate thinks? She says nothing, she looks at nothing, she's in some queer dream of her own. A more important question is, what do the police think? "

" I think they think I did it. First suspect the husband —isn't that natural? "

" You weren't Chilby's husband. "

" But they're looking for some connection between Daphne and Chilby. Heaven knows, they may find one. But there's this queer business of Daphne going straight from Chilby's cottage to see Thea Arkwright. The police told me about that. I've just been to see Thea. "

Roger stood still, taking a packet of cigarettes out of his pocket. He held it out to Marcus who gave a brief shake of his head, looking away with a desperation on his face that Roger, as he lit a cigarette for himself, did not seem to notice.

" Marcus, what do you know about that woman? " he asked.

" About Thea? "

" Yes. "

" Not a great deal, " Marcus said. " She's Meg's friend, more than mine. "

" But who is she, where did she come from, who was her husband? "

" I think her husband was in the Navy, or perhaps it was the Air Force. Anyway, I know he was killed in the Far East. I think she comes from London. At least she talks of London as if she'd lived there a good deal. "

" What brought her to East Shandon? "

" Just trying her hand at country life, the way people do. I shouldn't think myself she'd stay very long. "

" You say you know her husband was killed in the Far East. I suppose you mean that that's what she's told you. "

" Yes, I suppose I do. But why shouldn't it be true? "

" No reasons whatever, that I know of, " Roger said. " But she was badly scared about something this morning

133

—looked as if she hadn't slept any more than I had and talked about having no alibi for the time of either murder."

"Hysteria," Marcus said. "That sort of woman's often highly hysterical under the hard-boiled surface. Besides, she's the last person who's known to have seen Daphne alive."

"I don't think her motive for murdering Daphne is really quite powerful enough to be convincing," Roger said, "and I don't see that she's got any motive at all for murdering Chilby, unless she isn't the person that she seems."

"I agree, I agree," Marcus said. "Actually there isn't any question at all about who did the murders. It was Velden. Watertight alibis be damned. Chilby turns up and threatens him, Daphne listens in on the threats and finds out what they're all about, then both of them get murdered. Don't tell me that's just coincidence. I've always felt there was something wrong about the man and when Thea, after a drink or two, couldn't stop herself saying that he isn't all that he seems, even though she's in love with him, I know just what she means. Kate says positively he isn't an impostor—all right then, I'm prepared to believe that he isn't, but he's done something that gave Chilby a hold over him, a very terrible hold. Suppose, for instance, he murdered Miss Velden. Chilby dropped hints about that to us, asking about the inquest and so on. Actually I shouldn't be at all surprised if that's the true explanation, though I shan't be surprised either if it turns out that he's got a watertight alibi for her death too—not at all surprised. Alibis—I feel I can't say it too often or too definitely— simply don't impress me. Velden's our man, Roger, and for three murders, Miss Velden's, Daphne's and Chilby's."

"You're going just a little too fast for me," Roger said. "It seems to me just possible that some of that's open to question."

Marcus gave a slightly shamefaced grin.

" It was going just a bit fast for me myself," he admitted, " but that's what my mind's like. Plant an idea in it and it's got roots and branches before I know where I am. Shall I show you Chilby's room now? There's something rather curious about the way the thing happened that I'd like to show you."

Roger glanced towards the house. " Is Kate . . .?" he began, then changed his mind and said, " All right, let's go and take a look at it."

They went to the cottage.

The stone-floored sitting-room looked almost as it had when Meg first brought Chilby into it, except for a great many muddy footmarks between the door and the stairs. It was clear that Chilby had not used this room at all, perhaps because he would have had to go to the trouble of lighting a fire, whereas in the bedroom upstairs there was a plug for an electric radiator. But there was not much disorder in the bedroom either. The police had removed Chilby's belongings and but for the unmade bed and some unwashed crockery on the table, there were no signs left of the Jeacocks' first tenant.

Standing just inside the door, Marcus observed, " I don't suppose we'll ever be able to let the place now." There was a trace of satisfaction in his voice. " It won't really matter though, since I've given up smoking."

" What's the curious thing you mentioned? " Roger asked, pausing in the doorway, looking into the room over Marcus's shoulder.

" I'll show you in a moment. First of all, though, you're standing just about where the murderer stood when he took his shot at Chilby, so the police say. Angle of the shot and all that. Chilby was standing in the middle of the room. There's no sign of anyone having broken in downstairs, so unless the murderer had some-how got hold of a key, it seems probable that Chilby let him in, came upstairs ahead of him and was immediately shot from the doorway. Then——"

" Wait a minute! " Roger's tense pale face had hardened with suspicion. " Wait a minute. The key—what was that you said about a key? "

Marcus looked at him over his shoulder, then drew away from him.

" What about a key, Marcus? " Roger demanded.

" Nothing in particular," Marcus said. " Daphne had one, hadn't she? But they found it in her handbag, you know, in the car. Did the police ask you anything about it? "

" No."

" Then it doesn't sound as if it's specially important, does it? "

" I don't know. Duplicates can be made. I had that key in my possession for some weeks."

" Before you'd ever heard of the existence of Chilby."

A confused looked came into Roger's eyes. He gave his head a slight shake, as if to disentangle it from some sort of clinging web.

" Yes. I'm sorry, Marcus. That was an idea of mine sprouting roots and branches before I knew what it was. All that talk of yours downstairs about Velden—it sounded such nonsense—and then throwing out this thing about a key—it began to feel like a trap. I'm sorry. But the way you won't tell me what Kate thinks——"

" For heaven's sake, I haven't the faintest idea what she thinks! "

" You see, I said certain things to her when I saw her on Sunday morning, which could have sounded as if I were thinking—planning. . . . And she's got a fair amount of reason to distrust me anyhow. But if she thinks that I——"

" You know, what Kate thinks isn't really all that important," Marcus interrupted. " What the police think is. Now come over here. Come and look at this window."

He went to the window in the wall at right angles to the house next door and pointed.

Roger came to his side.

Marcus was pointing at the broken pane in the window of Kate's bedroom.

Roger looked at it silently for a little, then said, " Well? "

" The murderer smashed that window," Marcus said. " He leant out of this window and smashed it with a broom-handle. We found the broom up here. The police have taken it away with them. The murderer did it to prevent being seen from Kate's room, in the reflection in the window."

" Yes," Roger said impatiently, " I know about the reflection. Quite sensible of him, I should say. What's specially curious about it? "

" Well, how many people would you say knew about the way that reflection worked? "

Roger turned his back on the window. He walked away from it towards the door. Then he spun round again, facing Marcus.

" I did."

" Yes, and so did I and Meg and Kate and Thea and Velden. But who else? Oh, and I believe Miss Harbottle, and incidentally, she could have come here. She drove Meg and Kate home and neither of them can remember hearing her drive away before they got into the house. If she came to see Chilby then——"

Roger broke in with an irritated gesture, as if the implications of this were too fantastic for him.

" So your mind isn't quite made up about Velden," he said.

" Oh yes, it is. All the same . . ."

" I was right then that you didn't believe much of what you were saying."

" I never know quite how much I believe of what I say," Marcus said. " I only find that out later. But the point is, Roger, and it's an important point, if someone came into this room who hadn't been told about that trick, and there was no light on in the room next door,

137

so that the trick worked in the reverse direction, would it ever occur to him to break that window? "

Roger thought it over and shook his head. " I don't think so."

" Well then—and don't say I'm working round to accusing you of anything—that makes the circle of suspicion unpleasantly narrow, doesn't it? And of the people in that circle, who but Velden could be a murderer? "

" In spite of his alibis? "

" In spite of his alibis."

" What about Thea Arkwright? "

" The main thing against that is that she's the one person who didn't know that we'd all be out for the evening," Marcus said. " She left here to go to her affair in Carringdon before Miss Harbottle rang up to invite us to dinner, and after it she went to the cinema there with a friend, then went back to her bungalow. It was she who rang up the police, you know, when Velden went there to say that he'd discovered Daphne's body."

" All the same, that doesn't give her an alibi."

" Which in my view is to her credit," Marcus said. " Now come next door and see Kate. But, Roger——"

Roger looked at him with an apprehensive sort of eagerness, ready to wince if some nerve should be jabbed too sharply.

" She's stayed on here because of you," Marcus said. " I know that much. Now let's go."

They went downstairs and out into the cottage garden.

But Roger had no immediate chance to talk to Kate, because when they entered the sitting-room of the house next door, they found Richard Velden there.

He seemed put out at seeing Roger, muttered something at once about having only dropped in for a moment, then started towards the door. But something in the faces of the other two men seemed to strike him and he stood still, looking warily from one to the other, his slim body growing taut.

" So it's begun," he said softly. " The ganging up on the stranger."

Marcus, who felt there was perhaps a certain truth in the accusation, could not think of anything to say. Roger did not seem to think it necessary to say anything.

" That's what I came for this morning," Richard went on. " To put a toe in the water and find out how cold it is. Well, it's cold, very cold. So now I know where I am."

His face looked pale and blank, except that his eyelids looked even redder than usual, and for an instant there was a flash of furious anger in his eyes.

He turned to Kate, who, of all the people in the room, looked the most detached, almost as if she had not heard of any murder, but before he could speak to her, Meg said distractedly, " It's just that we're all very upset, Mr. Velden, and don't—well, certainly don't know where *we* are."

" Then perhaps I can help you a little." His voice was controlled, but pitched higher than usual. " I can see I make a good suspect. None of you knows me well. I came from God knows where and I wasn't wanted."

" And it happens, I think," Marcus said, " that you had met Chilby before."

" I can't stop you thinking it," Richard said.

" You still deny it? "

" Indeed I do."

"There was, if you remember, a certain phone call——"

" Ah, that telephone call. The call that gave me such a shock that in front of you all I made a real fool of myself. Ah yes, that call."

" It was from Chilby," Marcus said.

" Yes," Richard agreed, with a tight little smile on his lips. " It was from Chilby, whom I'd never heard of before, wanting to make an appointment with me. But it happened that Mrs. Cronan, who'd come into the

139

morning-room without my knowing it, was listening on the extension. She was not only listening, but she joined in the conversation. And it was what she said that gave me the shock—because she did know Chilby. But I don't think this is the time to tell you what she said."

He glanced at Roger as he said this, but Roger had turned away to the window.

" I'm sorry," Marcus said, " but I don't believe you."

Richard shrugged rather exaggeratedly.

" That doesn't surprise me. And I don't expect you to believe what I'm going to tell you now, but these are the facts. That talk on the telephone, as you saw, gave me quite a shock. I wanted to think it over before I saw Chilby, and I'd agreed to see him on Monday morning——"

" Not on Sunday evening at 7.30?" Marcus interrupted.

" No," Richard said, " on Monday morning, at the Priory. And I wanted to do some thinking first, a lot of thinking. So on Sunday morning I took the car and drove off. I like to drive when I've something to think out, but I meant to be gone only for three or four hours. Then for some reason I kept going, ending up in a pub in a place called Long Stampton about ten miles from Bath. I got drinking there with some men and in the end I stayed the night there, driving back early the next morning. That, I think, puts me a good long way from East Shandon at the time when Daphne Cronan was being murdered."

" A long way," Marcus agreed in an odd voice. " An astonishingly long way."

" And last night," Richard went on, as if he had not noticed the peculiar tone in which Marcus had spoken, " you know what I was doing. I left my own home around six o'clock, I think, or soon after. I went to see Elsie Wibley, stayed there a while, went on to the ferry, found Daphne's body, went on to Thea's bungalow, went back to the ferry, waited for the police and for Cronan, took them all back to the Priory, telephoned Miss Harbottle, waited for you, Jeacock. . . . Until long after Chilby had been killed, there are other people who can account for all my movements."

" That's true," Marcus said thoughtfully. " That's all perfectly true."

" So I shouldn't waste too much time and suspicion on me," Richard said, going to the door, " when they might do good work elsewhere."

He went out. From the window they saw him in the garden, walking quickly away, his small fair head held high and his arms swinging.

There was a silence in the room that he had left, then Kate got up quietly and went to Roger. She slipped an arm through his.

" Let's go for a short walk, Roger," she said rather timidly. " Meg and Marcus won't mind if we leave them for a little."

## CHAPTER XIV

WHEN ROGER LEFT Thea Arkwright's bungalow, Thea had sat for a minute or two looking at the doorway with her head bent to one side, as if she were listening for his return. When she had heard the slam of his car-door, she had stood up and gone to the window, and even after his car had disappeared up the lane, had stayed there, with an irresolute frown on her face. Her tension seemed to increase while she waited. Her breathing deepened. Then with an exclamation, she turned to the telephone.

But as she picked it up, she changed her mind and put it down again. Again she stood still, her lips starting to move in a hurried, silent argument with herself. She talked to herself a great deal when she was alone, nearly always like this, silently and with only slight twitching movements of her lips, as if she feared to have the habit discovered. With one hand balled into a fist, she struck it softly several times against the palm of the other, forcing home some point that she was making, then, still talking, she turned slowly and went to her bedroom.

Starting to dress, she pulled on a girdle and a pair of stockings, but interrupted herself to begin making the bed. With this job half-done, she stopped it and went to the dressing-table, taking a long and critical look at her face in the mirror. After that she went on with her dressing, but now was suddenly in a hurry, snatching a fresh blouse off a hanger, zipping up her tweed skirt, screwing a pair of large gilt ear-rings on to her ears, thrusting her feet into brogues and lacing them up, all with clumsy but swift impatient movements.

Her lips no longer moved, but were formidably pressed together. She left the room without having finished making the bed.

A quarter of an hour later her hand was lifted to the brass lion's head door-knocker on Miss Harbottle's front door. It was opened so promptly after Thea's first knock that it was plain that Maggie must have been lurking close to the door. She looked pleased to see Thea and told her that Miss Harbottle would be pleased to see her too, took her into the drawing-room, removed the brass fire-screen from the fire-place and set a match to the fire, talking all the time in excited unfinished little sentences about poor Mrs. Cronan and the probability that no one in East Shandon was safe in their beds.

She added that what with the deaths on the roads, railway accidents, floods, fires and even tornadoes, of all things, in Hertfordshire, of all places, you didn't know, when you went out, if you'd ever come home again.

" Still," she said, " we mustn't grumble."

" No," Thea agreed, " it doesn't do much good."

"That's right, we mustn't grumble," Maggie said. "That's what my mother always said to me, though things used to be different then, I sometimes think. Still, they could always be worse, so we mustn't grumble."

Miss Harbottle, coming in, said with a smile, " Maggie and I have both got very stiff upper lips. We do all our grumbling in an atmosphere of determined cheerfulness."

" A tornado," Maggie said, " in Hertfordshire. It came down and took the roofs off all the cottages and the bull got loose."

Thea's forehead puckered. " Has there been a tornado in Hertfordshire? "

" It was in the papers about three years ago," Miss Harbottle said. " It made a great impression on us. It's become our symbol for sudden alarming misfortune."

Maggie waved her little head several times and trotted out.

When she had gone, Miss Harbottle said, " Maggie was hoping we'd have a visitor. She's been badly needing someone to talk to. That's my fault, I'm afraid. I can stand only quite a little talk about murder. Do sit down, Mrs. Arkwright. That's what you've come to talk about, I suppose."

" I'm afraid it is." Thea sat down in a chair near to the smoke-filled fire-place. There was the same irresolution on her handsome bold face that there had been when she stood at her window, watching Roger drive away. " I need advice, Miss Harbottle. I need it badly."

" I give a great deal of advice," Miss Harbottle said. " How much of it is useful to the recipients I haven't the slightest idea, but still, when I'm asked for advice, I always give it. I can't control myself."

" I can't always control myself either," Thea said with a crooked smile.

" What is your trouble, Mrs. Arkwright? "

" I'm frightened," Thea said simply.

" So am I," Miss Harbottle said. " Fear is in the air around us. I think perhaps that it's always there, like one of those faint, unpleasant smells, the source of which one can't track down and which may be drains, and therefore a menace to the community, or which may be some hysterical sensitiveness of one's own nervous system, and therefore something which one should keep to oneself as much as possible."

" Mine's drains, then," Thea said.

" Are you sure? "

" Well, it's real enough. I've lied to the police, Miss Harbottle, and I know who the murderer is."

Miss Harbottle's eyebrows shot up, but there was something sceptical in the gaze that she kept on Thea's face.

" You know, of course, whether or not you've lied," she said.

" But you don't think I know the other thing. I could be wrong—one can always be wrong,—but it seems so clear . . ."

" Tell me first about your lies to the police."

" I lied about Daphne's visit to me. You know about that, don't you? "

Thea's hands were gripping the arms of her chair. They seemed to be holding her down in it, preventing her from changing her mind about asking for the advice that she had said she wanted and plunging out of the room.

" She came to see me on Sunday evening," she said, " straight after going to see that man Chilby. My first mistake was not to volunteer that information to the police before they asked me about it. I thought—it was a silly, muddled thing to think—that perhaps they wouldn't find out about it at all. My second mistake, when they asked me why she had come to see me, was to say she'd just dropped in for a drink. Of course they found out in no time that that's something she wouldn't have done, and putting that together with the fact that I'm the last person who's known to have seen her alive, they think—they may think—that's to say, I'm afraid they may think . . ."

" The worst," Miss Harbottle said. " I imagine they're given to thinking the worst, but of all of us, which leaves you in no special danger. But you want to tell me, I imagine, the real reason for Mrs. Cronan's visit."

" Yes, particularly since I've just been telling some more lies about it. That was to Roger. He came to see me this morning. He wanted to know why she'd come. I told him—well, just something stupid I made up on the spur of the moment about Daphne's having dropped dark hints about Richard Velden being an impostor."

" Why did you do that? " Miss Harbottle asked interestedly.

" Because I was afraid, afraid! "

" Of Mr. Cronan? "

" Yes."

" So he's your murderer."

" Well . . ."

The hands that had been anchoring Thea to her chair lost their grip. She sprang up, thrust her fists into the pockets of her tweed jacket and started walking feverishly up and down the room.

" Look at it like this," she said. " He hated her. He must have. She'd given him every reason a woman can give a man to make him hate you. . . . But that isn't where I meant to start. I meant to tell you about her coming to see me. She came straight from Chilby's cottage and she was white and shaking. She was in a state of absolute terror. She didn't say so, but she couldn't hide it. As a matter of fact, she didn't even tell me then where she'd just come from. I only found that out next day when I was at the Jeacocks', and it was after that that I started putting two and two together. You see, she hadn't seen Chilby himself, so it could hardly have been of him she was terrified. The only person she'd seen was Kate Hawthorne and that only for a few minutes. Kate hadn't followed her. But someone had followed her and that was the real reason why she'd dashed into my bungalow. She dashed in, hardly giving me time to get the door open, and then rushed straight to the window and pulled the curtains.

And she stayed for a while, talking in a wild incoherent way, gulping down the drinks I gave her, and trying to make up reasons for staying a bit longer. I wasn't awfully sympathetic, because I thought the whole thing was an act of some sort, and at last she went, looking—well, now I remember her as looking as if she might be going to her death. I didn't think of that at the time, I thought she'd just got fed up suddenly because she saw the scene wasn't working out as she'd intended. But now I think of the look there was in her eyes. . . . Well, it's no use talking about that now. It can't be altered. She went and that's the last anyone saw of her till she turned up in the river."

" And she never talked to you about Richard Velden being an impostor? " Miss Harbottle said.

" No."

" So you lied to Mr. Cronan rather more extensively than to the police."

" Not really. You can lie by leaving things out as much as by putting them in."

" Yes, indeed." Miss Harbottle had begun a rapid tap, tap on her knee with one finger. It was a delicate, tapered finger, but roughened by work in the garden. " What reason have you for assuming that it was Mr. Cronan who was lying in wait for her? "

" Who else could it have been? "

" Any one of several million people, I should think. You see, Mrs. Arkwright, you somehow have to connect Mrs. Cronan and Mr. Chilby. She went to see him, then was murdered, then he was murdered too. So to me it seems likely that they had met before, probably not in East Shandon, or even in Carringdon, but in some environment which contained certain other not very desirable people. And so——"

" No," Thea interrupted. Then she stood still and gave an uncertain shrug of her shoulders. " I don't know. You may be right. But I believe it was Roger—to which I'd like to add that even if it was, he has my sympathy and if I weren't afraid of him—no, perhaps even though I am afraid of him—I'm not going to take this story to the police unless you tell me to."

"Good gracious!" Miss Harbottle exclaimed, as if she had not been prepared to learn that this was to be her responsibility. "I can't possibly dictate your actions."

"You say you like to give advice."

"But without expecting it to be taken—believe me, without ever expecting it to be taken."

Thea gave a tight-lipped smile. "That rather surprises me. I should have expected you to have the courage of your convictions."

"I have fewer convictions than you seem to suppose."

"But what *am* I to do?" Thea's voice rose on to a thin, high note of strain. "If Roger had understood that I lied to the police mostly for his sake I think I'd just have gone on lying—because I think if there was ever anyone who deserved murdering, it was Daphne. While he still loved her, she made his life hell with her infidelities, then when he'd had enough of it and found someone else whom he could care for instead of her, she came back and wrecked that for him. Then, when she was sure she'd done that, she started to play around . . ." Her voice cracked and dried up.

"With Richard Velden," Miss Harbottle added. "I am quite abreast of all the gossip. And I think, Mrs. Arkwright, that you've now arrived at your real reason for coming to me for advice." She sounded a little gentler as she added, "Where does Richard fit into all this?"

"He doesn't!" Thea said fiercely.

"Yet Mr. Chilby appears to have come here with the object of seeing him?"

"Perhaps he did. Perhaps he came to tell him something about Daphne." Thea slumped into a chair again, looking for the moment moodily thoughtful rather than distraught. "Anyway, I understand Richard has two perfect alibis. It's a waste of time, trying to implicate him—thank God!"

" Are you going to marry him? "

" The subject so far hasn't come under discussion," Thea answered on a false note of flippancy. " If you rely on gossip, you're liable to get ahead of events." A look of pain clouded her eyes. " But it's pointless for me to try pretending, isn't it? I'm in love with him—of course I am. I've never known anyone like him. He's . . . But you don't want to hear about that."

" I can see," Miss Harbottle said, " that you might have great attractions for one another. You are very strongly contrasted. He has a fluid quicksilver quality, you have——"

" I know, I'm solid, stubborn, a bit stodgy! " Thea sprang up again and resumed her striding about the room. " And I'm older than he is and no great beauty."

" I was going to say, you have great tenacity of purpose and I suspect a great capacity for loyalty. That's something of which I never had a great deal, at least where my emotions were involved. That's partly why I've seldom yielded to them. As long as my head guides me I can maintain the appearance of a stability which I find morally attractive. Now I'm going to ask you a question. Why, since you tell me you've already lied to the police and to poor Roger Cronan, should I believe a single word of what you've told me? "

Thea looked blankly amazed.

" Don't you believe me? "

" I haven't made up my mind."

" Why should I have come here at all if I only intended to lie to you? "

" The answer to that might be that you wanted to shift suspicion from Richard to Roger."

" There's no need to do that. Richard's safe."

" In that case it would have to be your own safety that you were worrying about." But it did not sound like a challenge. It sounded as if the old woman were trying to work out all the possible meanings of Thea's actions without yet committing herself to accepting any particular explanation of them. " And that would mean, of course, that your account of Daphne's visit is quite untrue. And that—I can't help it—seems to me probable. I find your description of her behaviour extraordinarily unconvincing, I'm not sure why."

" I'm sorry," Thea said. She turned to the door. " I'm sorry I came."

" No, please don't take it like that," Miss Harbottle said. " My mind doesn't work very fast and you've given it a number of surprises."

" Anyway," Thea said, listening, " you've just got another visitor arriving. Maggie's having a good chat with him before she lets him get at you. So I'd better go." She broke off, her eyes glittering nervously as she recognised the voice of the man who was talking to Maggie in the hall. " It's that policeman—Inspector Wylie."

Miss Harbottle rose.

" Then you must decide rather quickly what you intend to tell him," she said. " I'm sorry I've been able to help you so little."

" I shan't tell him anything," Thea said. " I shall leave it as it was. If you won't believe me about Daphne's terror, I don't see why he should. And I don't want to do Roger any harm—almost less now than before. So perhaps after all it was a good thing to come and talk. Perhaps you have helped me."

She was putting a hand out to the door when it opened and Maggie announced Inspector Wylie.

Thea switched on a look of surprise to greet him, said that she supposed he had not come there to meet her, and left.

He came into the room, apologising for disturbing Miss Harbottle. The apology sounded curt and mechanical, a form of words that he used automatically, having long ago forgotten its meaning.

He looked, as he spoke, as if his mind might be on something far removed from the murders, not, however, on anything particularly pleasant. It might have been a bill that he could not see his way to paying, or some slight pain that was worrying him more than he wanted to admit.

Miss Harbottle, attending to the fire, which was still mainly smoke, asked him how he thought she could help him.

" I believe you've lived here in East Shandon a long time," he said. It sounded as if he were making conversation, to keep his mind off his private worry.

" Thirty years," she said. " Some people would call that a long time, but you'll find there are some old people in East Shandon who look on me practically as a newcomer."

" Yes," he said, " I know them. I've been trying to talk to some of them. When it comes to facts—a few simple facts about dates and about people—it's difficult to get anywhere with them."

" So you've come to me." She gave a sigh. " D'you know, there are some days when this fire won't do anything but smoke. I don't know if it's the direction of the wind, or the way the fire's been laid, or a bird in the chimney. Thirty years in this house and I still haven't got to the bottom of it. I've been told that the only way to get a chimney like this swept properly is with a gooseberry bush tied on to a pole. But I'm a Londoner really. Many things about country life still baffle me. Whom do you want me to tell you about? "

" You were acquainted with Mrs. Cronan, I believe," Wylie said.

" Yes, I knew her, but not very well. Since she and her husband settled in Carringdon, I've met her perhaps a dozen times, mostly in other people's houses, though I have had her and her husband to dinner here, an invitation which I don't much blame her for not returning. There could have been nothing very attractive to her in the relationship."

" Do you know her husband any better? "

" A little. As you certainly know by now, there was a time when it seemed probable that he would divorce his wife and marry Katherine Hawthorne, whom I've known since she was a child. At that time I did my best to find out what I could about him, particularly as Miss Velden, who thought of herself as responsible for the girl, was likely to be very upset, when she heard about it, by the turn events had taken. She was a good kind woman, but extremely conventional out of sheer nervousness. My view of Mr. Cronan at that time, and it hasn't altered since, was that he is a pleasant and sensitive man, a little too gentle for his own good, sincerely in love with Miss Hawthorne, but burdened with a rather unnecessary sense of responsibility, not only towards his wife, but towards Miss Hawthorne too and her youth and inexperience. The result of this sense of responsibility, I'm afraid, was that he treated Miss Hawthorne with considerable cruelty. I'm sure, however, that it was unintentional and that he suffered even more himself. A great pity, all of it. I'd made up my mind to tell Miss Velden that I thought he would make Miss Hawthorne a very good husband and I should have done so if she hadn't died so suddenly."

" Ah," Wylie said.

He seemed to think that this sound was enough to prompt Miss Harbottle to go on talking, but watching him with a questioning look on her face, she waited.

" Miss Velden . . ." he said after a moment.

" Yes? " Her tone was the same as before, but her thin tall body looked suddenly more angular.

" You did know her well," he stated.

" I did."

" You were perhaps her closest friend."

" I think so."

" Then I have some news for you which I'm afraid

may distress you." His face was set as if that inward pain had just given him a specially severe twinge, " As a result of obtaining certain information about her sudden death, I've to-day applied for an exhumation order."

# CHAPTER XV

" So it's come to that."

Miss Harbottle spoke quietly. Her squared shoulders relaxed. She did not look particularly surprised.

Wylie shed his apparent preoccupation.

" You've been expecting it? "

" No, only dreading it," she answered, " and blaming myself for the violence of my imagination. Now that I know it isn't simply my own private nightmare, I feel rather better. But what led you to take this action? Local gossip only, or something more concrete? "

" Mainly two pieces of information, one from Mr. Kirby, Miss Velden's lawyer, and one from Miss Wibley, her cook. Neither appears to know the fact supplied by the other, or to be aware of the implications of what was told to me."

" Mr. Kirby is a very reliable man," Miss Harbottle said. " Miss Wibley would be completely honest about any material thing, but might find it difficult not to add a tinge of colour to her recollections."

" I've checked up on what she told me with Dr. Benson, who attended Miss Velden," Wylie said. " She was taken ill late in the evening of Sunday, March the seventeenth. She was alone in the house at the time. Miss Wibley and the housemaid both had Sunday afternoon off and Miss Hawthorne had gone out with Mr. Cronan. Miss Velden had had the cold supper left ready for her by Miss Wibley, then, as she often did when she was alone, had gone to bed with a book. She was taken ill in bed, tried to get up to go downstairs to telephone for the doctor, but collapsed before she had even reached the door of her room. Miss Wibley, coming in at ten o'clock, heard her moaning and went to her assistance. Miss Velden told her at once to send for the doctor, telling her that she had been unable to reach the telephone. When the doctor came, Miss Velden told him the same thing. Yet at about half past nine that evening, Miss Velden telephoned her lawyer at his private address and told him that she believed herself to be very ill, that she had just destroyed her will and wanted to see him next day to make a new one. As you know, she died before the morning and the new will was never made. You remember also that there was an epidemic of gastric 'flu at the time, and Dr. Benson had no hesitation in signing her death certificate. He and Mr. Kirby never met or considered that the times at which they had received those telephone calls were of any importance."

Miss Harbottle gave a long sigh.

" Then it was not Christina who telephoned Mr. Kirby," she said.

" That seems certain," Wylie answered.

" Yet he knew her quite well. Not intimately, perhaps, but he'd handled her affairs over many years and would, I think, have recognised her voice."

" A voice can be imitated."

" Particularly easily, I suppose, on the telephone." She dropped her eyes to her hands, which lay loosely folded in her lap. " You know, I imagine, that Richard Velden was once on the stage."

" I know that, yes. And he's the person who benefited by his aunt's death. But it happens that he can prove that he was on tour in Canada at the time."

" Is that absolutely certain? "

" I think so."

" A pity."

" You don't like him? "

" Not a great deal. But I said that because it follows

153

that you must have turned your suspicions to someone whom I do like."

" Miss Hawthorne," he said, as if in reply to this, " might have a motive for murdering her aunt. But I can't think of any reason why she should then telephone Mr. Kirby and destroy Miss Velden's will, in order to get herself disinherited."

" Good," Miss Harbottle said. " I was a little afraid, from the look of you, that you might be one of those over-subtle people who find simple facts very hard to accept."

Wylie's far-away look immediately returned.

" *Simple* facts? " he said, as if he not only found them hard to accept, but altogether doubted their existence.

" Nevertheless," she said, " it's very satisfying to be subtle and I'm sure that if we were to allow ourselves to speculate now as subtly as we're able, we should soon be able to break Richard Velden's alibi."

" That's what Mr. Jeacock seems to believe," he said. " But my speculating, such as it is, has led me to a different conclusion."

" Conclusion? " she said sharply.

" I'm sorry, that wasn't the right word. I haven't arrived at any conclusion."

" But your speculations . . .? "

He rubbed one cheek reflectively. " I don't think I'd discuss them yet if there weren't some more questions I'd like to ask you. They're about Mr. Cronan and Miss Hawthorne mainly—and Mrs. Cronan. As you said just now, I'd heard of the divorce and so on—something about it at any rate. But what I haven't got at all clear in my mind are the dates when it all happened. When did Mrs. Cronan leave her husband? When did he meet Miss Hawthorne? When did his wife return? When, in the middle of it all, did Miss Velden die? I expect you know all these things."

" Yes—or I did. My memory isn't what it was." Her

voice had hardened. " But what bearing can they have on the possible murder of my old friend? "

" I could tell you more about that when I know the answers. If the dates aren't as I suppose them to be, they'll have no bearing on it."

" Well then . . ." She closed her eyes for a moment. " As I remember it, Mrs. Cronan left her husband about Christmas time. That's stuck in my mind because it seemed to me somehow particularly heartless of her to leave him just then, though that's doubtless a foolish way of looking at it. At least it saved him the expense of buying her a Christmas present."

" May I ask how you heard about it? "

" Mrs. Arkwright told me. I remember that distinctly. She hadn't been living here very long and I remember how impressed I was at the speed with which she'd learnt the essential facts about us all."

He smiled at her tone. " Some people have the gift."

" You've found her useful, perhaps."

" I'm not sure. Now about Mr. Cronan . . .? "

" Mr. Cronan and his meeting with Miss Hawthorne," she said. " Let me see, I think that happened almost immediately. Miss Velden wanted to make some alterations at the Priory and asked him to advise on them. Say it was early in January."

" And Mrs. Cronan's return? That was *after* Miss Velden's death, wasn't it? "

Her eyes snapped open. They caught the look of intense interest, on Wylie's face.

In a low voice she said, " But what you're suggesting is something *horrible*."

" Is it? " He looked preoccupied with his secret troubles once more, with that pain, or whatever it was, that he did not dare to mention.

" Conspiracy," Miss Harbottle said. " Conspiracy between Roger Cronan and his wife to murder Christina Velden and then to rob Katherine Hawthorne—God knows, perhaps to murder her too! "

155

" You haven't told me yet if Mrs. Cronan returned to her husband before or after Miss Velden's death," he said.

" It was after," she said grimly.

" Long after? "

" No—no, that was the heartbreaking part of it for poor Katherine.  Only a few days."

" In fact, as soon as it was known that she had not inherited Miss Velden's fortune? "

She did not reply, but he seemed to feel no need to repeat the question.

A moment afterwards he said, " As I told you, I haven't arrived at any conclusion.  But there's a possible case there, if you assume that somebody else realised what was happening, destroyed the will and made the call to Mr. Kirby, somebody who came on the scene too late to save Miss Velden, but wanted to make sure that the Cronans' plan should miscarry."

" Do you mean Katherine?  Could that be whom you mean? "

He waited and soon she went on, " You're either a very fanciful person, or a very observant one—because there's a dreadful sort of sense in your suggestion.  I mean that the character of Katherine herself makes it not quite impossible.  Not quite.  But let me make it clear that I don't believe it for a moment."

" I'm a long way from believing it myself yet," he said.

" I wish I felt sure of that.  This suggestion of yours . . ."

" Wasn't it your suggestion, Miss Harbottle? "

" Don't pretend you didn't put it into my mind.  This suggestion that it could have been Katherine who deliberately disinherited herself, as a sort of revenge for Christina's murder. . . . But that would mean that she herself suspected murder and said nothing about it! "

" Well? "

" This is shocking! " she exclaimed.  " You're putting thoughts into my head, words into my mouth . . ."

" Or have they always been there? "

Her body had sagged and her eyes were frightened.

" The poor child—could it be possible? *Could* it? Carrying a load like that in silence because she'd loved him, yet seen through his horrible scheme and prevented its succeeding—I believe she'd be capable of it. For one thing, she bore her debt of gratitude to Christina very uneasily. That was mostly Christina's fault, because in spite of all her good intentions, she couldn't give the child the warmth she needed, and at one moment asked too much of her and at the next too little. And I've sometimes thought that Katherine felt the loss of her inheritance as a kind of liberation. Not that that's how it will strike her when she's older and looks back on what she might have had. But still, I believe that now she'd almost be capable. . . . No!" A grim little smile brightened her face. " No, I don't know how you've led me into saying all these things. That telephone call to Mr. Kirby was made by someone who knew that Miss Velden was upstairs in her room, in pain and dying. This person made the call and never went to her assistance. Of that Katherine would not have been capable."

As if he had merely been waiting for her to reach this conclusion by herself, he said, " Do you think that Mrs. Cronan would have been capable of it? "

" I don't understand," she said. " Why should she do it if she and her husband had conspired together to do the murder and to get the money? "

" But I believe the idea of conspiracy was your own," he said.

" *My* idea? "

" Wasn't it? "

" Perhaps it was, perhaps it was. This is dreadful. Yes, it was I who first mentioned it. You're suggesting now, however, that Mrs. Cronan was not a party to the murder, but somehow found out about it and realising that if she was to be able to return to her husband, she must prevent Katherine inheriting a fortune, she made the call to Mr. Kirby and destroyed the will. After that she would have had a powerful threat to use on her husband and that would have led eventually to her own murder. I admit I *like* that suggestion better, Inspector. But it's still too fanciful, isn't it, too complicated? On the whole I find it easier to believe that Richard Velden's alibis are false."

"You do?" His tone was level. "Well, I must thank you for a very helpful talk. But there's just one thing more I'd like to ask you. Do you happen to know what Mrs. Cronan's name was before her marriage, or where she came from?"

"Her name I believe was Lackley, or Lackland or something like that," Miss Harbottle said. "I saw it on the flyleaf of a book her husband lent me. And I think she came from somewhere in the Midlands. I know she often spoke of Birmingham as if she'd lived there."

"Lackley," he said, "or Lackland."

"Or something like that."

"Something beginning with an L."

"So far as I remember."

"Not a V? Not by any chance a V?"

She shook her head.

"And so far as you know," he said, "had she ever been in America?"

"You're looking for some connection between her and Richard Velden."

"Yes. If only her initials had ever been D.V. . . . But I suppose that must stand for Dick Velden. Unless . . ." A startled look came into his eyes.

"I don't know," Miss Harbottle answered. "So many people have been to America, haven't they? But I can't remember her ever speaking about it. You have other means of finding these things out."

"Yes, but short-cuts are sometimes useful." He stood up. He was still looking startled and was suddenly in a hurry to be gone, but he paused to ask, "Have you heard the curious fact about the broken window?"

"No."

He told her quickly about the broken window of Kate's

bedroom, explaining how it narrowed the field of suspects. Then he left.

Miss Harbottle saw him to the door and when she had closed it behind him, suddenly leant against it. Her eyes had closed and her breath came unevenly as she listened to his heavy footsteps crunching on the gravel of the drive. Maggie, who had been waiting for this moment and had come trotting into the hall from the kitchen, her little head thrust forward in excitement from between her bowed shoulders, gave a gasp of concern.

The fear of death was very strong in Maggie. It was not her own death that she feared, but that of Miss Harbottle. A great terror often possessed her that at any time now she might be left, not unprovided for, of which she knew there was no risk, but alone and unwanted.

But to speak of this fear, to admit it, was to make it worse, so while doing as much as was humanly possible to protect and coddle Miss Harbottle, Maggie usually spoke as if the main worry on her mind was the problem of what would happen to Miss Harbottle when there was no one to look after her.

" Look at you! " Maggie exclaimed now. " Look at you wearing yourself out, driving around the country after dark, staying up half the night, seeing visitors, doing a lot too much talking and using up your strength. You ought to have more sense by now, dear, you really ought. As it is, I've got to have the sense for both of us and one day I shan't be here. Now come along—come along and sit down and I'll bring you a little glass of brandy."

But Miss Harbottle had recovered herself.

" Did you say talking too much? " she said. " That's what I've been doing. Talking far too much. I wonder if I've done any harm by it."

" Never mind about that," Maggie said. " Come and sit down and I'll bring you a little glass of brandy."

" Tea, please, Maggie. I'd far sooner have tea."

Miss Harbottle went back to the drawing-room. She

picked up the telephone and gave the Jeacocks' number. Meg answered her.

" Good morning, Margaret," Miss Harbottle said. " Katherine is still with you, I believe. May I speak to her? "

" She's still staying with us, Miss Harbottle," Meg answered, " but she's just gone out with Roger."

" With——? " It sounded as if Miss Harbottle had not heard.

" With Roger Cronan," Meg repeated. " They've gone out for a walk together."

" I see. Thank you."

Miss Harbottle put the telephone down.

When Maggie came back to the drawing-room with the tea, she found the room empty. Looking round it in dismay, she heard the old car chugging away down the drive.

# CHAPTER XVI

WHEN KATE and Roger left the Jeacocks' house together, they had walked for several minutes without saying a word. Kate had kept her arm linked through Roger's. He had let it rest there, but awkwardly, with no response at all to its light pressure. He seemed so unaware of her and of where they were going that she might have been leading a blind man.

Yet it was Roger who spoke first. " You shouldn't have done this."

" Why not? " she asked.

" Because I'm going to be arrested for murder."

" And I'm your motive? And a murderer and his motive shouldn't be seen together? "

" You can put it like that."

" Only I don't expect anyone will see us. And even if they do . . ."

" Well? " There was a kind of antagonism in his voice.

She looked up at the sky. The wind was driving the clouds across it, shaping them into masses of lighter or darker grey, leaving here and there between them a small ragged patch of blue. The air smelled moist, as if there were more rain coming.

" Well," she said, " they'll have to get used to it sooner or later."

He glanced at her quickly. " If you mean that——"

" No, wait! " she said. " I want to say something first. And it's an awfully difficult and complicated thing to say. It's a sort of confession. If—if you don't mind hearing it."

" If you're going to tell me that you think I'm a murderer, that's something I think I've got to get used to."

" Don't," she said. " Please don't. It's got nothing to do with that."

" On the other hand," he said, " if it's just a rush of loyalty to the head, because I'm in trouble, I think I'd sooner do without it."

" Don't, don't, don't! " she said. " I only want to tell you about something I did long ago—because of something I thought long ago. Ages ago. Anyway, that's what it seems now. A whole year ago, Roger. Long before anyone thought of murder."

" Before anyone thought of murder," he repeated after her. " For that, my dear, you'd have to go a long way farther back than a year."

She gave her head a shake. " I mean when my aunt died."

" I'd thought of murder long before that," he answered. " Years before. I don't know when I first began to think of it, it's so long ago. I thought of car smashes, blunt instruments, poisons, gas leaks——"

" Stop it! " Her thin long fingers dug into his arm. She stood still, pulling him round to face her. " I know what you mean, but this isn't the time to say things like that. You'll go to pieces if you do. You'll go out of your mind."

His eyes met hers now, but still looked blind.

" You don't know what I mean," he said.

" I do," she said. " I didn't before, but I do now. Since we talked yesterday I've been coming to understand it. And if I'd let you talk to me when it all happened— I mean, when my aunt died and Daphne came back to you—I might have understood it then. I'm not sure that I should have, I was such an idiot, but I might have. In time I might have, even if I'd been slow. I've been horribly slow, Roger, trying to make sense of it all. That's what I want to tell you about."

He said stubbornly, " I wanted to murder Daphne. I had the thought in my mind I don't know how often."

" And what did you really do about it? Took great care of her, tried to look after her———"

" But thought of her dying! "

" Of course, of course, and thought of the other things too. I know you hated her and wanted to be free of her and cared for her too and tried to do your best about it all. But I didn't know that *then*—I couldn't understand any of it at all and I thought—this is the awful part, because this was real and not just the sort of nightmare you've got on your mind—I thought, you see, it must be the money."

Her face had gone very white while she was speaking. She moved a little away from him.

" Ah yes, I knew that," he said. " As it all happened, you couldn't have helped thinking that, could you? "

" Didn't you hate me? "

" Hate? " His gaze was clear now. The blind look had gone. " I'd no hate to spare for you. And we're talking too much about hate, aren't we? "

" Yes, much too much. But let me finish. You remember that evening we spent together, that last evening."

" Yes, I remember it." He smiled. It seemed to Kate a long time since she had seen him smile. " Sometimes I tried to forget it, but it had a way of coming back."

" Then I went home," she said, " and the doctor was there, and a nurse, and Aunt Chris was dying. But she still knew who I was then and she could speak a little. And she asked me to give you up, she tried to make me promise, but I wouldn't and she told me I'd regret it, and that's almost the last thing she ever said. I cried about it a lot, because it seemed such a shabby finish between us. Neither of us had really been like that, distrustful and unkind and bullying. We'd loved each other very much in a sort of a way, only at the end it somehow didn't work out and so we let each other down in that terrible way. Then I found her will——"

" You *found* it! " he exclaimed.

"Yes, it was half-burnt in the morning-room fire-place. So I finished burning it, because I thought that was what she'd want. And then—then Daphne came back and you let her stay."

He started to say something, stopped, then reached for her and drew her close to him. After a little while they turned and started walking back towards the Jeacocks' house.

A light shower came on as they went, whipped into their faces by the wind. Each started to speak several times, but with the words half-spoken, forgot what the rest were to have been.

They were nearly back at the house before Roger said, " But it isn't all simple yet. I think you'll find I'm supposed to be a murderer."

" Just so long as you don't suppose so yourself! "

" Or you."

" I never did." She laughed. " I only thought you were a swindler and seducer."

" I'm puzzled," he said. " There's some change in you, some change in the way you look, only I can't put a name to it."

Kate looked as if she thought that she could put a name to it but did not choose to do so, and perhaps to have said just then, as they walked through the rain,

163

still under their private cloud of fear, that she was feeling the warm breath of happiness, would not have been appropriate.

When they reached the house they found Meg, Thea and Miss Harbottle in the sitting-room.

Meg and Miss Harbottle were side by side on the sofa. They were not actually holding each other's hands, but in their attitudes there was something that suggested a clinging together for support.

Thea sat in a chair half-turned away from the other two women, as if she had chosen to isolate herself with problems of her own. She was the only one of them who had not turned her head to stare apprehensively at the door at the sound of Kate's and Roger's arrival.

Of Marcus there was no sign. Nor was there any sound of his typewriter from upstairs.

Miss Harbottle was the first to speak. " Katherine," she said, " I came to see you. I had a great shock this morning and I felt it was urgent to tell you of it. I've already spoken of it to Margaret and Mrs. Arkwright, but they will bear with me, I think if I repeat it. Mr. Cronan, I'm glad that you're here too."

Both Roger and Kate looked at her uncomprehendingly. Neither of their minds seemed to focus upon her. They stood together in the doorway in serene and unapproachable gravity.

Her eyes went quickly from one face to the other, then she glanced significantly at Meg.

" In the circumstances, I think it may be advisable if I talk in words of one syllable," she said. " The police believe Christina Velden was murdered."

That brought them only partly out of their trance. Turning to each other, they tried to read her meaning in each other's faces.

She went on, " I was a little surprised not to find the police here before me. On the chance that I might get here first, I came as quickly as I could to warn you about the way their minds seem to be working. I have to say too, with great regret, that I probably assisted their minds to work in that manner. I'm extremely sorry about it, extremely. Given a little skilful prompting, I said some incredibly foolish things."

Thea interrupted hoarsely, " Where *have* they gone? "

She swung round in her chair as she said it, to stare with hard eyes at the old woman.

" I imagine into Carringdon, in the expectation of finding Mr. Cronan at home," Miss Harbottle said. " It didn't occur to them to look for him here."

" But why should they want me about—about the murder of Miss Velden? " Roger said confusedly. " If it was a murder."

" They don't—that's the answer," Thea said. " That detective led Miss Harbottle on to talk about you and Kate, to see if she knew anything herself about the way it all happened, but it's Richard they're after. Can't you all see that? " Her eyes were haunted. " They've made their minds up it's Richard and somehow they'll work it so that it comes to look as if it must have been. He hasn't a chance. Only I shan't believe it. Whatever the rest of you swallow, I shan't believe it."

" You're quite wrong, Mrs. Arkwright," Miss Harbottle said. " Inspector Wylie told me that Richard was in Canada at the time of Miss Velden's death. The inspector's approach to the problem was imaginative but not mystical. He showed no signs of believing that a human being can be in two places at once."

" But where does Roger come in? " Kate asked. " How could he? "

" I'll tell you that in a moment," Miss Harbottle said. " But first I'm going to ask you to do something that may be painful, Katherine. I should like you to tell us all what you can remember of the evening when Christina was taken ill."

Before Kate could answer, Meg said miserably, " I wish Marcus were here. I can't think where he's disappeared to. He'd want to hear it all. And he might be able to—I mean, sometimes he's very—that's to say, he's quite clever sometimes."

" Oh, he's brilliant, he's a genius! " Thea said bitterly. " With him to help, we could certainly tie the noose round Richard's neck."

" Katherine," Miss Harbottle said.

" Yes," Kate answered, coming farther into the room and sitting down on the edge of the chair, looking scared and lost. " I'll tell you all that I can remember." Her glance went to Roger. " About the will and all."

" The will? " Miss Harbottle exclaimed.

" Yes, tell them about that," Roger said as he went to stand behind Kate's chair.

" But I'll have to begin farther back," Kate said, " with Aunt Christina finding out about Roger and me. I never knew for certain how she found out and of course it doesn't matter now. We weren't trying very hard to keep her in the dark, and I suppose half the village knew about it in any case, but I'd hoped that she needn't know until Roger's divorce was through. She'd have worried less then—at least, I thought so. But I never realised how very much she was going to worry when she did hear, so perhaps that was wrong."

" It wasn't I who told her," Miss Harbottle said, " if that's perhaps what you've thought."

" No, I didn't think that," Kate said. " And it doesn't matter now. I think whoever it was must have spoken to her after church that morning. There'd been nothing unusual about her at breakfast and she went off to church quite happily, so far as I could tell. I didn't go with her and I didn't see her until lunch-time, because when she came in she went straight up to her room. There was nothing unusual in that. But at lunch she hardly spoke to me and she hardly ate anything. I asked her if she didn't feel well and she answered that she was perfectly well. Later, of course, I thought that couldn't have been true, but now . . ." She looked questioningly at Miss Harbottle. " If it wasn't 'flu, but poisoning . . . Because that's what you mean, isn't it? That she was poisoned."

"Yes," Miss Harbottle said. "And from what Inspector Wylie told me, it sounds most probable that the poison, if there was poison, was in the food that Elsie left ready on a tray for Christina's supper."

"So at lunch it must just have been worry," Kate said. "The worry of what she'd been told about me."

"And she may have been told rather more than was true," Miss Harbottle said.

"You can bet on that!" Thea said. "Or if not, you can bet she added the details herself. People do, in my experience."

Kate flushed.

"I don't know exactly what she'd been told," she said. "She went up to her room again after lunch and I didn't see her until the late afternoon, just a little while before I went out to meet Roger. We were going to the pictures in Carringdon. I'd told Aunt Chris I was going to the pictures, but I hadn't told her I was going with Roger. She came downstairs and asked me if I wasn't going with him and I admitted it then. So then she asked me a lot of questions about my feelings for him and I told her everything. And she cried a little and told me she'd never dreamt anything like that would happen to me. The whole idea of a divorce upset her and she begged me to break off with him. But I told her I wouldn't and I went out. I met Roger, we went to the pictures and had supper together afterwards. I told him then that Aunt Chris knew about us and that she seemed to be very upset——"

"One moment," Miss Harbottle said. "You say she was upset. Does that mean she was angry?"

"Just very unhappy," Kate said.

"Did she speak of her will?"

"No."

"She didn't tell you that unless you broke off your relationship with Mr. Cronan she'd change her will?"

"She said nothing about that. But it's what she must

have had in mind when she spoke to me, because after I'd gone out she rang up Mr. Kirby and told him that she was going to change it. He told me about that afterwards. And that evening I found the will——"

"*Found* it?" Meg and Miss Harbottle exclaimed together, as Roger had exclaimed before them.

"Yes, half-burnt in the morning-room fire-place."

"But you never said a word about this before," Meg said. "What did you do with it?"

"I finished burning it," Kate said. "You see, what I thought had happened was that she'd set it alight there and telephoned Mr. Kirby, but by the time she'd done that had been feeling so ill that she'd gone straight upstairs and hadn't noticed that the will hadn't got burnt up. I don't mean I thought that straight away, because I didn't know anything about her having telephoned Mr. Kirby, but I did realise that she'd meant to destroy her will. And I thought, of course, that it was because of my having refused to break off with Roger."

"So you finished the job for her!" Thea sounded thunderstruck.

"It didn't make any difference," Kate said. "The fact that it was half-burnt and that she'd telephoned Mr. Kirby would have shown what she wanted."

"Only she didn't telephone Mr. Kirby," Miss Harbottle said. "That call was made when Christina was upstairs in her room, too ill to get downstairs to the telephone to call the doctor. And the will, I think, must have been left half-burnt because whoever had set a light to it didn't dare to linger a moment longer than necessary in that room, knowing that you or Elsie Wibley might return at any moment. Where did Christina keep the will? Do you know that, Katherine?"

"She kept most of her more important papers in the bureau in the morning-room," Kate said.

"Locked up?"

"Oh, I don't think so. There was nothing particularly private—just the usual things, the title deeds of the house, an old passport, her birth-certificate and so on. It was all very tidy and businesslike and easy to sort out."

" And the morning-room has a door straight into the garden," Miss Harbottle said, " which, so far as I remember, was hardly ever locked except at night or when the house was empty."

Meg jumped up.

" Where *is* Marcus? " she said helplessly. " I wish he'd come."

" Too bad he's missing it all," Thea said dryly. " But I'm afraid, Miss Harbottle, there's something in all this that I don't understand."

She stood up too and planted herself, looking solid and formidable, in front of the old woman.

" Who was supposed to gain by all this will-burning and telephoning? " she asked. " No, wait! I know what you're going to say—Richard. But Richard was in Canada. All right then, who else could have wanted Kate disinherited? Because that's what it comes to, doesn't it? Richard got the money, so the murder wasn't done by someone who wanted the money. But the only other outcome of the murder was that Kate, instead of being a young woman with great expectations, became penniless. Or could it be that all this business with the will was camouflage? It has to be one or the other, doesn't it? "

" Camouflage? " Miss Harbottle said. " Of what? I can't imagine any conceivable reason for the murder of poor Christina—if it was a murder—other than her money. *Something* to do with her money. It was not a murder of sudden violence, but was carefully planned. It can't possibly be shuffled off on to any stray burglar or mere homicidal maniac. It was done by someone who knew her ways and her house. And I can't believe that it could have been the outcome of any sheer hatred of Christina herself. She was not a person who roused strong feelings in others. She was liked and respected, or else possibly mildly disliked and despised, by the people who knew her, according to their own temperaments. But she was never much loved or much hated."

Thea nodded her head in vigorous agreement.

" So that brings us back to what I said first, doesn't it? " she said. " Miss Velden was murdered not by someone who wanted her money, but who wanted to make sure that Kate shouldn't get it."

" But who could that be? " Meg asked.

" I'm sorry," Thea said, " I think there's only one answer. Daphne Cronan."

Roger gave a little sigh, as if he had been waiting for it. Miss Harbottle shot a swift glance at him. Kate reached for his hand and held on to it.

" Isn't that the answer, Roger? " Thea said. She did not look pleased with what she was saying. Her face was flushed and embarrassed. " Daphne told Miss Velden about you and Kate, then did the rest of it, thinking that if there wasn't any money you'd lose some of your enthusiasm for divorce and remarriage. And then——"

" Then I murdered Daphne for revenge," Roger said. " And Chilby—why did I murder Chilby? Because he'd seen me? "

From the doorway a voice spoke, " Is that a confession? Have I arrived just in time to hear the murderer confess? How very dramatic."

As they all looked round, startled, Richard Velden strolled into the room.

" I'm sorry, Mrs. Jeacock," he said. " I knocked, but no one came, yet I knew you were all here, because I heard your voices."

He was smiling and his voice was light, but his slight body was tense and his eyes, as he looked round at them all, were wary and on the defensive.

" Don't let me interrupt you," he said to Roger. " I only came to see if I could help in any way."

Miss Harbottle was frowning, as if his tone offended her.

" No doubt you came here after you'd been visited by

Inspector Wylie," she said. " He did come to see you this morning, I assume."

" You assume wrong," he said.

" But then where did he go when he left me? " she demanded. " He didn't come here, he didn't go to you. If he'd gone to Mr. Cronan's house, he'd have found no one in——"

" And where's Marcus? " Meg repeated. " I do wish I knew."

" Perhaps they're holed up together somewhere," Richard suggested. " In the police station, for instance. I should think a police station's quite a likely place in which to find a policeman."

Miss Harbottle rose. She was still frowning and her voice was colder.

" I shouldn't, after all, be surprised if you were right," she said. " My question was a foolish one. The police station." She went towards the door. But she stopped before she reached it. " Margaret," she said, turning to Meg, " I've been told about a window that was broken last night. Inspector Wylie explained to me how the fact that it had been broken narrowed the field of suspects to —yes, to the people who are in this room. I confess I didn't entirely understand him. Perhaps that was because I didn't quite succeed in visualising the scene. I wonder if you would be so good now, before I go home, as to let me see it."

" Of course," Meg said.

Horror had dawned in her face while Miss Harbottle was speaking. Up to that moment it seemed not to have occurred to her that her sitting-room contained a murderer. Looking glad to escape from it, she started to the door, and led the way up the stairs.

" Actually," Miss Harbottle said as she followed her, " that remark of mine was not entirely accurate. For one thing . . ." But she did not finish what she had been about to say.

" For one thing," Meg said, " Kate and I have alibis

for the whole evening, and Thea didn't know we were all going to be out, and you yourself . . ." She stopped in confusion.

"Good gracious me," Miss Harbottle said. "Yes, of course. I drove you home, I was on the spot. That serves me right. I'd been talking as if I myself were above suspicion. What a mistake."

"But I didn't mean. . . . Oh dear, I suppose I did though," Meg said. "I've been doing a ghastly kind of mental arithmetic about us all ever since we found him last night. And feeling that it was all really my own fault, for letting the cottage to him. I'll never do anything like that again without consulting Marcus."

She opened the door of Kate's bedroom.

The window with the broken pane was open. A cold breeze had driven the rain in. One of the yellow and white curtains was wet and there was a spray of raindrops on the windowsill.

"To see how it worked before it was broken," Meg said, "you can use a mirror."

She picked up the hand-mirror from the dressing-table. Miss Harbottle took it and thrust it out through the window, holding it where the pane of glass had been.

She gave a gasp. In the mirror she had seen a face. It was a sallow face which she had recognised instantly, though it had been distorted by a ferocity that she had never seen on it before, while the eyes that had met hers glowed with frenzied excitement.

"Marcus!"

The mirror slipped out of her fingers and smashed on the ground below.

# CHAPTER XVII

IN THE COTTAGE bedroom Marcus tried to pull himself together. The crash of the glass and the faint cry from the window had broken in on the almost trance-like state in which he had spent the last half hour. For a shocked moment he wondered how long he had been under observation and what he might have done during that time that it would be dreadful to him to have known.

Trance-like states were not at all unusual in Marcus, but he generally took great care to enjoy them in private. The occasions when he seemed to be lifted out of himself on a great wave of imaginative excitement, when his mind was no longer quite master in its own house, but started splitting into any number of different parts, each of which entered into and took over the control of some personality wholly unlike his own, were normally allowed to occur only in his own study.

There he was safe from interruption because no one could approach the door without his hearing footsteps on the stairs and in the passage.

But he had thought himself alone in the cottage bedroom. Although he had gone there to think about the broken window, he had forgotten that it might be of interest just then to others besides himself. That was unlike him. The most probable cause of his forgetfulness, he thought, as he halted a dramatic dash forward into the room from the doorway, was the fact that he had not had a cigarette for about sixteen hours. The strain was beginning to tell on him, producing absentmindedness and muddle.

That dash forward from the doorway had been a re-enactment, perhaps the eleventh or twelfth re-enactment,

173

of what the murderer had done in this room the evening before.

With each repetition a part of Marcus's mind had become more deeply identified with the murderer. First walking up the stairs, then standing still in the doorway from which the police believed the shot had been fired, then holding out a hand with a fountain-pen threateningly clenched in it and muttering, " Bang, bang! " and then darting forward towards the window, looking round for something long enough to reach the open window of the room next door, Marcus's workaday self had had less and less to do with his actions.

Up to a point it had all been plain sailing. The submergence of his mind in the murderer's had come easily enough. The meeting with Chilby at the door downstairs, the few words spoken—" All right then, I'll come up for a few minutes—there's just something I want to say to you in private "—the walk up the stairs with Chilby in front, the shot from the doorway, these had soon made a pattern so clear in Marcus's mind that at a later time he would find it difficult to remember that he had not actually witnessed them. But after the shot came confusion.

Why, when you came to think of it, had the murderer broken the window?

It had not been to prevent the murder itself being observed from Kate's bedroom window. The doorway could not be seen from the window. The murderer could have shot Chilby and gone downstairs again without ever coming within the range of vision of a watcher in the house next door.

So it must have been necessary for the murderer to remain in the room after the murder and to move about in it where he could be seen. Probably he had been searching for something, as Daphne Cronan had searched before him. But knowing, as she had not, how the window of the adjoining room would present a reflection of him searching to anyone in that room, the murderer had first broken the window.

And that, as Marcus had already pointed out to Roger, made it certain that the murderer was one of a small group of people who had been told of that property of the window.

But there had been no one in the room next door. There had been no one in the house. The Jeacocks and Kate Hawthorne had been dining with Miss Harbottle.

Yet for some reason the murderer had feared their return.

That was where the confusion arose in Marcus's mind and why, as he made his murderous entry to the room and followed it by the dash forward to the window, his imaginings did not flow on smoothly in harmony with those of the murderer. Something blocked him. What his reasoning and his intention should have been as he rushed forward remained obscure to him.

Then, just as he met Miss Harbottle's amazed stare in the hand-mirror, he suddenly knew the answer. He knew into whose identity he had been struggling to find a way and in the excitement of it he made the most frightful face at Miss Harbottle.

A moment later he was his normal self, petrified with embarrassment at the thought that perhaps all his play-acting had been watched by the old lady. At the same time, while one hand strayed instinctively to an empty pocket in search of a cigarette, he was already asking himself another question.

" All right, that's *who* it is—there's no question about it—but *why*? Why ever should that person need to murder Daphne or Chilby? "

His frustrated hand came out of his pocket and scratched his head violently. Muttering to himself, he went downstairs and out into the garden.

There he met Meg and Miss Harbottle, who had just come hurrying out of the house. Meg went to pick up the broken pieces of looking-glass.

" Margaret," Miss Harbottle said, looking uneasily at Marcus, " have you ever asked yourself if you are married to a maniac? "

" Who hasn't? " Meg said.

" Just so long as you aren't frightened of the answer! "

Meg looked at her husband. " What on earth were you doing? "

" Just thinking," he answered self-consciously. " I've been trying to enter into the mind of the murderer. Asking myself the question why, if I'd been the murderer, I'd have bothered to break the window when there was no one at home here. And so I've discovered who the murderer is. That's quite easy. Only it's an answer that makes it rather difficult for me to make up my mind why either of the murders should have been committed at all. There *is* a quite simple answer to that, of course, and it may be the real one. In fact, I suppose it must be."

" Would you mind telling us what you're talking about? " Miss Harbottle said.

" About who the murderer is," he said.

" So much I had realised, but you seemed to be continuing from there without troubling to clear that little matter up for us."

" Oh," he said. " Yes. Well, it's Thea."

" Oh, Marcus, don't talk nonsense," Meg said. " This isn't a game."

" A game, a game! " he cried. " You call it a game when I've been burning myself up with the effort of arriving at an answer, driving myself at it like an unwilling horse at a jump that he's deadly scared of, sending my imagination out into the dark places of the human spirit. A game! Well, it *is* Thea. Plainly. She was the only one of the people who knew about the window at all who didn't also know that you and I and Kate were going to be out for the evening. That's why she broke the window. She could see when she arrived that there was no one at home, because there weren't any lights in the house, but she didn't know that we mightn't come back at any time."

" And so she broke the window," Miss Harbottle said thoughtfully. " That's quite ingenious."

" It's more than ingenious," Marcus said irritably. " It's the truth. I'll go in and ask her about it."

" And be told, I'm afraid," Miss Harbottle said, " that you've left a few things unexplained."

" Of course I have," Marcus said, " but we'll get at them all in time. I never liked that woman. If Meg had only listened to me——"

" If I'd listened to you," Meg said, " we'd have no friends at all."

" Wouldn't that be better than having the place cluttered up with murderers and murdered bodies? Come along, I'm going to ask her if she didn't murder those two because Velden wanted it. If you assume that he and she are lovers, that seems quite possible. And it explains why he has such perfect alibis for the times of both murders. And it means that in a sense I was right from the start and he is the murderer."

Meg turned helplessly to Miss Harbottle.

" He doesn't know about the other murder," she said.

Marcus had already taken a couple of swift strides towards the house, but the words stopped him. He looked wonderingly from one woman to the other.

Miss Harbottle told him, " The police are going to exhume Christina Velden's body. There's some evidence that she may have been poisoned."

The half-clowning manner that Marcus had adopted during the last few minutes to help him over his embarrassed fear that his antics in the cottage had had an audience, and an audience as sharp-tongued as Miss Harbottle could often be, dropped from him. He put a hand on Meg's shoulder.

" This is true? " he asked.

" I'm afraid so," Miss Harbottle said.

" Yes, of course it's true that they're going to exhume

her—but true that she was poisoned, do you think? "

She told him rapidly what Wylie had told her.

" But this changes everything, doesn't it? " he muttered when she had finished. " It couldn't have been Thea who did that. Not, that's to say, unless she was something quite out of the way as a clairvoyante."

" Yes, to have murdered an old woman in the vague hope of later marrying the unknown man who was going to inherit her property would have been rather over-optimistic, and so far no other possible motive has suggested itself to me."

" So I'll have to think again. All the same, that was a nice point about the window. And it must mean something, even if I haven't got it quite right. Or perhaps I have got it right, and . . . But I should never have stopped concentrating on Velden. Three alibis for three murders is too much of a good thing. And now his motives for all three are crystal-clear. He murdered Miss Velden to get her money. He murdered Chilby, who somehow knew of this and turned up to blackmail him. And he murdered Daphne Cronan because she overheard something on the telephone and mixed herself up in it. That's logical and plain. And when you remember that at the time on Sunday evening when Velden claims to have been in a pub near Bath, he had an appointment here with Chilby, I think we can be morally certain that he's the murderer."

" An appointment here? " Miss Harbottle said. " That's the first I've heard of it."

" Chilby had it written down in a diary," Marcus said. " ' 7.30—D.V.' That is, Dick Velden."

" But——" Miss Harbottle began excitedly, then snapped her mouth shut.

" And it proves, doesn't it, that he must have known Velden before," Marcus said, " which Velden has all along denied."

" But Marcus! " Meg wailed suddenly. " You do talk such nonsense! *He wasn't here!* He was in Canada

178

when Miss Velden died. He was in a pub near Bath when Daphne died. And he was fishing Daphne's body out of the river when Chilby died. Those are facts. So unless he did it by magic, he didn't murder anybody."

The voice of Inspector Wylie joined in the conversation. Accompanied by Sergeant Wall, he had come soft-footed across the grass while Meg was speaking. " He might have used a guided missile."

Marcus flushed hotly.

" I've not been joking," he said. " I'm entirely serious."

Miss Harbottle's mouth twisted in a curious tight-lipped smile. " So, I believe, is the inspector. A guided missile. Dear me, yes, of course. I'd been wondering where you were, Inspector."

" Looking for something," he said.

" ' D.V.,' " she murmured. " So that's why you asked me this morning whether I knew of any connection between Daphne Cronan and Richard Velden."

" Yes."

" A guided missile," she repeated. " How interesting."

" I should prefer it myself," Marcus said in an offended tone, " if we went on talking about magic. There's nothing ridiculous about magic. But to bring in guided missiles at this stage seems to me most misguided humour."

" This guided missile isn't funny or fantastic," Inspector Wylie answered without a trace of amusement on his face or in his voice, but only that air which suggested that he was absorbed with some inner pain, a pain so unpleasant and persistent that if after all it was not cancer it could only be some remorseless moral pain, from which he was doomed to suffer eternally. " It's one that murderers have been using, I imagine, ever since men learnt to go on two feet."

179

He turned towards the door, muttering something in his constrained voice about getting it over.

They followed him into the house.

Kate and Roger, Thea and Richard were still in the sitting-room. Kate was still in the same chair in which she had been sitting when Meg and Miss Harbottle had left the room. She looked almost as if she might not have moved since they left. Roger was standing near her. He was looking down at her, absorbed in her nearness.

Thea and Richard were standing side by side at the window. She had an arm possessively through his. They seemed to have been watching the group at the window and to have been talking together in low voices, which ceased when Wylie came in at the door. Richard's face was whiter than usual and his eyes seemed prominent and staring. There was something restive and apprehensive in his pose and an unwillingness in the way that he suffered Thea to cling to his arm.

It was at Richard that Wylie looked when he came into the room. He looked at him without speaking. He had a piece of paper in his hand, which he held in such a way that Richard could see what was on it.

It was Richard who spoke first, in a high brittle voice. " So you've got it sorted out, have you? "

" I think so," Wylie said.

" Are you sure? Are you so very sure? "

Thea gave a moan. " Don't—don't say anything! You haven't got to say anything. Tell him so, Inspector. Don't you have to tell him that he isn't compelled to say anything? "

Richard snatched his arm out of her grasp. His lips curled back from his teeth in a rigid grimace.

" You fool! " he said. " D'you think that's going to work now? "

She raised her voice. " Be quiet! Don't say anything. He can't prove anything against you."

" Can't he? " Richard said and laughed. " What a fool you are, my darling! What a fool you've always been. He can prove it all so easily—can't you, Inspector? A telephone call or two, a copy of a certain certificate and there you are."

" Richard, Richard! " she shrieked. " Be quiet! "

" It's too late to be quiet," he said. " The time for that was long ago. I wanted to be quiet then, remember? I didn't mind my quiet life as a third-rate actor. I didn't want to change. I could go my own way then without getting pushed around any more than the other fellows. That's what I liked—I tried to tell you that. ' Don't push me around,' I said. But would you listen? And even now you don't see it's time to stop. You think you can still do it, don't you?—push me right up the steps to the gallows! "

" You're mad! " she cried. " Inspector, he's mad, he doesn't know what he's saying."

Wylie looked as if he thought so too, but Richard went on. " I know it's the end, and it's the end that I always knew would come sooner or later. They only had to find out one thing, as Chilby did somehow in America, and it didn't matter any more how good my alibis were. They'd know then, just as he did, who killed the old woman and why. And I'm glad it's come at last. I couldn't have stood it much longer, living in that house with that old woman's ghost and getting pushed around all the time, told every damned thing I'd got to do, down to turning another old woman out of her cottage, to squeeze a few more miserable pounds of the loot. It's the end and thank God it's the end! Look at that paper he's holding? Don't you know what it is, Dot? "

She turned her head stiffly towards Wylie, looking across the room at the paper in his hand. It was the copy of a marriage certificate.

As she did so, Wylie began, " Dorothea Velden, I arrest you——"

But there was a gun now in Richard's hand and the shots from it drowned Wylie's words. He sent three shots into Thea.

ELIZABETH FERRARS

The fourth shot went into his own brain.

Just before he fired it, he said, almost casually, "You can all say where I was for this one."

## CHAPTER XVIII

MARCUS SAID AFTERWARDS that he had been right all along. Here and there, he said, some of the details might not have been clear to him, but given another few minutes to himself, he would have had it all.

If at the last moment Wylie had not interrupted with his deliberately misleading talk about a guided missile, but had said accomplice, which was what he had really meant, he would not have been able to claim all for himself the triumph of discovering the murderer. In any case, it had been Marcus's insistence from the first, so Marcus himself asserted, that three perfect alibis are no proof of innocence that had led to the swift unmasking of the criminals.

Meg answered that so far as she was concerned Inspector Wylie was welcome to this particular triumph, that what she wanted was to be able to forget the whole affair as quickly as possible and that this would only have been hindered if Marcus had achieved too complete a success.

Marcus thought this over and decided to make no comment on it.

Returning to the way that the inspector had so unfairly confused him, he pointed out that he had been under the two great disadvantages of a sleepless night and sixteen hours without a cigarette.

"But I'll beat it," he said, "I'll get over it. All you need is strength of mind."

"But is it really worth it?" Meg asked dubiously.

"It's worth two pounds thirteen shillings and eightpence a week," Marcus said. "Untaxed."

" But if it's going to confuse your mind . . ."

" Only temporarily," Marcus said and turned to the stairs.

As if to prove that the worst of the confusion had already sorted itself out, the sound presently reached Meg of his customary hop-skip-and-jump typewriting.

Of the people who had been present when Richard Velden paid his score of fear and hatred, only Miss Harbottle had maintained a calm of mind which had made it possible for her to question Inspector Wylie closely on certain points that had continued to puzzle her.

To Maggie, when she arrived home later that day, she said, " No, Maggie, don't fuss—I'm feeling much better than I was this morning. The tornado has gone back to Hertfordshire and the bull, after all, didn't get loose. I would like that cup of tea I missed, but let's keep the brandy for when we really need it."

" That's all very well," Maggie said, " but some people aren't as young as they used to be."

" Oh, my dear, if you'd like a little brandy yourself," Miss Harbottle said, " you're welcome to it."

In the end the two old women sat down in the kitchen, where there was a better fire than in the drawing-room, and had a very small glass of brandy each.

" Of course, if anyone had told me how the D.V. was written in that man Chilby's diary," Miss Harbottle said presently, feeling relaxed and thoughtful, " I'd have guessed the solution straight away. I always thought of Mrs. Arkwright as Dorothea. These names like Kate and Meg and Thea always seem to me so inferior to the names they're short for. I don't suppose I should call even you Maggie if it weren't somehow impossible to call you by your real name. I wonder whatever possessed your parents to call you Magdalen."

" I never heard for sure," Maggie said, " unless it was something to do with their spending Bank Holiday once in Oxford. It's a nice-sounding name, I've always thought, but nobody's ever called me by it. . . . But the cheek of it! " she added.

She meant Dorothea Velden's long and patient masquerade in the village, and to say that something was cheek was almost the worst thing that Maggie ever said of anybody.

" Well, it was hearing me speaking of everyone by their proper names," Miss Harbottle went on, " that made Inspector Wylie think of Mrs. Arkwright as a possible Dorothea Velden, and guess the reason for Mrs. Cronan's visit to her. And that made him think that the evidence that Mrs. Cronan had obtained in Mr. Chilby's room, was probably hidden in her car, since from the fact that Mr. Chilby's room was searched after his death, it seemed plain that Mrs. Cronan had not parted with it to the murderer. It was Mrs. Arkwright, of course, who was to have visited Mr. Chilby at seven-thirty on the Sunday evening. It was then, and not the next night, that she intended to murder him. That's why she sent Richard Velden so far away. It was to be utterly impossible for him to be thought of as the murderer. But just when she must have been preparing to set out, all her plans were upset by the arrival of Mrs. Cronan. She came, I suppose, to challenge her with being secretly married to Richard. She was in love with him herself and having overheard Mr. Chilby's first blackmailing threat on the telephone, searched his flat and found a copy of the marriage certificate, it was natural, I suppose, for her to go and abuse the woman who it turned out was actually in possession. I don't suppose her intentions went farther than that. I never thought of her as a particularly intelligent woman and I don't imagine she suspected the murder of Miss Velden. If she had, I dare say she'd have been more cautious about going to the bungalow alone. Yet she did take Chilby's gun with her, and she didn't tell Dorothea Velden that she'd brought the marriage certificate away with her and left it hidden under one of the cushions in the car. If she had, it would never have been left there for the police to find and Dorothea Velden would not have searched for it the next evening, when she effected the murder of the man Chilby."

Maggie had not tried to follow this, any more than Miss Harbottle had expected that she would.

" Play-acting! " she said. " Living among us like that, joining the Women's Institute, helping at the church sale of work and all! The cheek of it! "

" Yes, she was an actress," Miss Harbottle said. " She'd met Richard and married him when she was on tour in America. But apparently she didn't like the life as well as her husband did. She came here, took that bungalow at Miss Velden's gates and cultivated her acquaintance, all with the object of murdering her so that Richard could inherit her fortune. And it must have been she who told Miss Velden about Katherine and Mr. Cronan after church that Sunday morning, choosing a Sunday, of course, because she knew the servants would be out and supper waiting on a tray and perhaps even that Katherine was to be out too. And it was she who imitated Miss Velden's voice on the telephone. I suppose she told poor Christina about Katherine's love affair to precipitate a scene of some sort, so that Katherine shouldn't be too surprised at finding herself disinherited and start asking dangerous questions. And then the woman waited. Waited all these months, so that her husband's second courtship of her and their remarriage shouldn't seem too suspiciously swift. . . . You know, Maggie, I told her I thought she had great tenacity of purpose and a great capacity for loyalty—though perhaps loyalty isn't quite the right word for it. She had, indeed she had. But she had to relieve the tension of waiting by those evenings I'm told she used to spend in the Rising Sun, when she talked a little too much about Richard Velden. Then having talked too much, she did her best to turn it into a rumour that he wasn't the real Richard, which could always safely be disproved. . . . But I'm talking too much myself."

" It does you good," Maggie said. " Now you'd better go upstairs and have a lay down. I put a hot-water bottle ready in your bed for you."

" A hot-water bottle! " Miss Harbottle exclaimed. " Good gracious, I think the afternoon's going to turn out quite fine. I shall go out and start pruning the roses. I noticed Mrs. Jeacock has done hers already."

The sun was shining, as she spoke, through a rift in the clouds that was part of a pattern of clear rainwashed blue, spreading across the sky.

Kate and Roger, twenty miles away on the downs, felt the warmth of the sun on their faces as they stood looking at the dappling of light and shadow that moved across the country below them.

" I've a feeling about him," Kate was saying, " as if he mightn't have been all as bad as he seemed. I think he hated it all—what he'd done and the trap he'd got into and being so mean to silly old Elsie. And I believe he meant it when he offered some sort of reparation to me. I can't know that, of course, but that's how I felt about it when he spoke of it. I thought he meant it." She paused, then added, " I'm glad he got out of it by himself."

Meg Jeacock had much the same thought in her mind as, coming out of the house with some crusts of bread in her hand, she started tearing them up and scattering them on the lawn. Richard's final action had been kind to all of them, for it was finished now, the whole tragedy, instead of still hanging over them for weeks to come.

As usual, the sparrows came around her first. Then the robin appeared, not so quick, but bolder, when he came, than all the rest of them. Then came a female chaffinch, more cautious of the sparrows than of Meg. But all of a sudden they all rose from the ground and darted into the trees and the hedges, complaining excitedly at some interruption. Meg turned to see what had alarmed them and saw a young woman walking towards her from the gate.

She was a girl of twenty-two or -three, with wind-blown brown hair and big gentle eyes. She wore a tweed coat that swung in loose folds from her shoulders. Full as it was, it did not conceal the fact that she was soon to have a baby. She smiled shyly at Meg.

" I'm sorry to bother you," she said, " but I've been told you've a cottage to let."

Meg looked at her in astonishment.

" Well, we have," she said. " But haven't you heard . . .? "

" About the murder? Yes, that's why I came," the girl said. " I mean—oh, I don't mean it like that. But I thought—you see, I thought you might have difficulty letting it again and so perhaps you just might be willing —you see, we've looked everywhere, John and I, for somewhere to live, but people take one look at me and see I'm going to have a baby and immediately say they're so sorry but the place is let already. And we can't stay with his family any more—we just can't, we can't bear it! And we can't buy a house because we haven't the money for the deposit, and we haven't any furniture, and so——" The breathless sentences stopped. She sounded close to tears.

" Well," Meg said uncertainly, then before she said any more, she suddenly went close to the door of the house and stood there a moment, listening.

To the girl it was an action that seemed strangely furtive, but as the reassuring starting and stopping of the typewriter upstairs reached her, Meg turned back to her and smiled.

" Well, it is to let," Meg said, " only it's really very small and the furniture—well, to tell the truth, we only put in a few odds and ends so that we could call it a furnished cottage and be able to get rid of the tenants if they weren't suitable. Of course, we could lend you a few more things——"

"But the rent?" the girl said. "Really it's only the rent that matters."

"The rent," Meg said, "is just two pounds thirteen shillings and eightpence a week." She thought for a moment, seeing the delight dawn in the girl's face, and added, "But you can have it for two pounds a week if you like it."

## THE END

188

>>> If you've enjoyed this book and would like to discover more great vintage crime and thriller titles, as well as the most exciting crime and thriller authors writing today, visit: >>>

## The Murder Room
**Where Criminal Minds Meet**

themurderroom.com